1'200

Amber .J Saunders

Chapter 1

One day, of a warm august, the start of university for
most, there was not much around, just a few small
houses down a leaf covered road, when a small cab drove
down. It had strange, inaudible music blaring from it,
and a very entertaining driver heading down this small
road. In the back of the cab sat a young girl in black
jeans, a blue vest top, and a purple shirt. It was a boy's
shirt but it suited her. She was pale with brown hair
around shoulder length, but tied up in a bun that was
falling apart, she also had a pair of white earphones in
but the left earphone was out. Additionally, she had a
pair of thick black glasses on a string around her neck.
She looked out the window watching the world go by,
until the driver spoke up over the music. "SO YOU'RE
GOIN' TO WestBrook RIGHT?!" He then turned the music
down so he could hear the passenger's response.
"Yeah" she replied, she was quiet, her voice not high and
yet not very low it, was obvious from her voice she was
British.
"Cool, what are ya studyin'?" He asked
"Media and dramatic studies"
"Cool, what course set you down for?"
"Twilight"
"Really? I didn't think many peepz still took the twilight
set! Haha, wow, yer in for a hell of a time!"
"I guess.."
"So, do you know what sort a dorm yer meant to be in?"
"It's meant to be this double unisex thing?"
"Really? Then where the hell's yer boyfriend?"
"Non-existent"
"Oh sorry, I didn't know you were that kinda girl..."
"I'm not; I just... thought it would be different. I'm used
to it though."
"What? How could you have lived like that all the time, a

boy and girl being roommates!? I wouldn't cope with that!"

"Well, I'm used to guys. When my mum died I became the only woman in my house so... Yeah I'm used to it."

"Alright, but a double unisex and twilight course? Hahah, wow, yer in for it girl!"

"Thanks...”

After a few more miles, the cab stopped in front of a large brick gate with lots of other people getting out of cars and saying goodbye to their families. This girl looked odd, the only girl in a taxi and the only one without any family, but no one really noticed. Some men in purple t-shirts came with the name "WestBrook" inscribed on their tops to unpack the back of the cab, but the girl took a few things like a laptop bag and put it carefully over her shoulder, a small but fully packed back pack and put only one side over her shoulder. The men looked at the bags and went off to deliver them to her room after gazing at a clip board. The gate however looked old, and the girl stepped through the crowds of crying mothers and stressing teens, just walking right into the gates. The brick was old but still had some colouring to it, it may have once read Westbrook on the top but it was now faded and unreadable. She walked past the gates with disinterest, while there were lots of people all doing different things, from people with a million bags, to others with only one. The surroundings were simple: A few trees, lots of buildings, nothing special, at the end of a small path was a white table, with people stood at it. She walked over and stood the other side from a rather fat man who looked a few years older than her.

"Name?" He requested in an inviting but tired tone. He had clearly been saying it all day.

"Luna Redgrave...” She answered

"Course set?" he asked

"Twilight." Luna wasn't sure why he really needed to know that, there could only be one Luna Redgrave, it wasn't a very common name. He fiddled with a clipboard, and then proceeded to grab some paper work from about half way down the large pile.

"Okay, Luna Redgrave on twilight set in a double unisex dorm" The man then officially stated.

"Yep, that should be me." She replied, feigning cheerfulness.

He handed her the paper work, it wasn't much but it was quite heavy. When she managed to manoeuvre the paper, so she could easily hold it in her hand, he then passed her a chain with two keys, a whistle, a plastic tag with the words L.R as well as a number on it, and a small sort of elastic spring thing. She took it and used the elastic spring to turn the key into a bracelet.

"Thanks"

"You know, most kids who come for double unisex come with their boyfriends..." he said bluntly

"Well, I don't have one." She answered back

"You're lucky though, only one guy was doing a twilight set and he was happy to be in a double unisex dorm. I haven't seen him yet but you're either really lucky or in really big trouble. I mean twilight sets are for five years."

"I know but the real fact is if he can put with me, and I don't want to kill him, I don't really care, heh."

"Cool."

She then walked away, looking at the paperwork to see where she was. She wondered around for a while just trying to find her dorm, having now put all but her map and dorm sheet in her backpack. Every building looked identical and the map was basically useless. Staring down at the map for a minute with her glasses on her nose... thump! Someone had crashed into her, sending her and them tumbling to the grass. She holds her head for a second, before opening her eyes to see who had hit her. It was a boy, he looked really young, a foot taller than her. He had quite neat blonde hair, which shone in the overseeing light. He was wearing a pair of blue jeans and a grey t-shirt that was slightly covered by a white over shirt. He also had a black back pack on, as well as matching black glasses that had been knocked off-centre by the collision. When he adjusted them, he gazed with wide eyes for a second. "A-a-a-are you okay?" He stuttered. He had a British accent and an all-round beautiful voice.

"I'm fine, just a little lost I think" Luna replied

The boy swallowed before speaking again "So am I."

"Really..?   Where are you going?" She asked.

"Hu..." he trailed off, looking down at his piece of paper on his lap.

"Well I'm trying to find-" Luna also looked down at her paper before continuing. "Dorm block B"

"So am I" They both said in sync. "It says I'm on floor 12" The boy clarified.

"I'm room 67 though..." She then raised her arm, showing the key and its door number.

"So am I!" he replied also holding up his arm he had also used the small plastic string to attach it to his wrist with the same number on it

"That can't be right" the both said before shifting to their knee's to compare sheets but it was they were roommates he then stuck out his arm and then spoke "Isaac Richards"

"Luna Redgrave"

they then shock hands and helped each other up and walking off in a possible direction by the map after a little while they found it and got to their room it was quite small it had two double beds side by side with only a small table separating them, two desks and chairs each leaning one side of the wall it had a bathroom with a bath shower and a toilet and sink the door it the bathroom was on one side if the wall next to the main door there was a tv on the wall in the centre of the two beds   with large tall bookshelves on either side. All their belongings had just been thrown on a bed each. the wall that separated the bathroom from the rest of the room had a large double wardrobe and at the other end of the room was a balcony looking out on to the road and a lake in the park across the street, all the walls where cream and the curtains where dark brown which matched the bed spreads provided next to the balcony doors was a small excuse for a kitchen with a washing machine a dryer a small worktop and a cooker there was three plug sockets behind the bed side table in the centre two at each desk and three in the kitchen area. it was a poor excuse for a room but neither of them really minded that much both where more concerned about that fact all their belongings hand simply been thrown on the beds the bed closest to the wardrobe had all of Luna's boxes and bags piled on it and the other had all Isaac's on it they stood in silence for a minute before Isaac spoke up "well it could be a lot worse"

"I guess you're right, but it could have been much better for a twilight set" she replied

"I know but im not complaining as far as im concerned it has a bed, a tv, a cooker and a place to charge my laptop I have all I need to be very happy" he laughed

they then both laughed before starting to unpack a bag at a time Luna started with clothes she didn't have very many just a few pairs of jeans a few leggings and skirt sets, a pair of shorts, two unused dresses , a few pairs of shoes mainly converses and flats and one pair of heels like the dresses seemingly UN used, two pairs of pyjama pants without tops and around 30 different t-shirts with different logo's for games, movies and music, the same amount of underwear sets and a couple of jackets of all sorts and styles. All laid out rather untidily in one side of the wardrobe Isaac had even less just jeans, t-shirts, jackets, shoes and underwear that was all. When all the clothes had been put away Isaac stood on the outer side of the bed looking around his stuff and so did Luna if they were to look up their eyes would have met in the middle it was odd the strange silence till Luna broke it

"So... Isaac what are you studying"

"Media and dramatic studies, you?" he answered

"Same" she said

"You know that's really getting odd like they matched up in a computer or something" he joked

"I know right it's almost creepy" she laughed

After that they both went back to looking for specific bags without unpacking anything

"You know what would be good" he asked

"What" she asked in return

"We could play like twenty questions to you know get to know each other a little better if we are effectively gunna be living together for like five years" he laughed

"Sure you go first Isaac" she said

"Uh ok... what is you star sign?" he asked

"Really?" Luna laughed

"Yes I'm serious, what are you?" he asked again

"Virgo .you?" she said

"Tartus" he answered

"Really" she asked

"Yeah" he answered

They both then returned to silence for few minutes till Isaac his phone from his backpack it was a rather beaten up phone and put it on the centre table

he then walked back and started sorting out movies and books both of them unpacking almost in sync every film the other had as well as books so much it had become a game between them almost competing on who could out do the other "now I bet you don't have this book" she then got out a very feminine book the perfect rom com in book from and to her surprise Isaac also got from his box a copy of it "what, no way you have read that" she said

"I have, my sister dared me to read it and I just like it that's all" he answered

Luna just laughed at him for a moment "it's not funny you like lots of guy stuff so what if I like a few more girly books and movies" he said

"Nothing it's just really odd that we are this alike" she
laughed

"I know, are you an actress, am I on a like hidden
camera show" he then began looking around for camera's
but had no luck "okay no camera's but I still think this is
weird"

"I know what's next you gunna tell me you like vintage
gaming too" she joked

"Yes" he answered

they then got a few boxes both full of different game
consoles from a originals to bran new consoles all
different per box and all similar games new and old just
standing there for a while just looking at the room the
whole place was almost symmetrical at the moment
before they both sat on the now clear space on their beds
just looking around "this is just two weird" they just both
kept saying till there was a loud knock at the door and a
high pitch voice shout "HELLO ,HELLO DARLING IT'S
ME ITS ANTI JULIA" Luna looked at the door in horror
for a second before leaping to her feet "Isaac if she asks
I'm not here" she said

"Okay" he said sounding very confused

Luna then ran into the bathroom and shut the door

"I KNOW YOUR IN THERE DARLING I CAN SMELL
VINTAGE CONSOLES, RECORDS AND BOOKS DEAR I
KNOW IT'S YOU OPEN THE DOOR DARLING" the voice
said

Isaac stood for a second confused before opening the
door to see this small around 37 year old woman in high
heels and a tight fitting yellow dress her hair was bleach
blonde with a pink streak in the front she almost jumped
on him as he opened the door before realising it wasn't
Luna "OH DEAR YOU MUST BE ISAAC BY LOVELY
NIECES ROOM MATE" she said

"I guess" he answered a tad confused

"OH SPLENDID" she then stood up and kissed him on

the check before wondering into the room her lipstick now stuck on his face

"So uh, what did you want then" he asked

" WELL DEAR I CAME TO SEE LUNA AND TO MEET YOU I   AM A TEACHER HERE I TEACH FASHION STUDIES BUT YOU WOULDN'T KNOW MUCH ABOUT THAT AS A BOY NOW WOULD YOU AND I WANTED TO SAY-"

She was cut off by Luna unfortunately sneezing in the bathroom and having her aunt find her pulling her out into the main bit of the room

"OH DEAREST, HOW ARE YOU I HAVEN'T SEEN YOU IN YEARS HOW BIG YOU'VE GOTTEN I CANT BELIEVE IT OH BUT YOU HAVEN'T CHANGED A BIT DEAR" she shouted hugging her and kissing her repeatedly Isaac just quietly giggled at her before shc stopped and pulled him close to her on one side "OH I CAN JUST TELL BY THE CHEMISTRY IN HERE YOU TWO ARE GOING TO GET ALONG SWIMMINGLY, I CAN JUST TELL MY LOVELY NIECE AND SUCH A LOVELY GENTLEMEN.. NOW I WANTED TO SAY DEAREST THAT YOU KNOW LUNA I HAVE ALLAYS BEEN A MOTHER TO YOU I LOVE YOU AS MUCH AS MY OWN CHILDREN AND ISAAC I WILL BECOME YOUR MOTHER TWO IF YOU NEED ME BUT YOU KNOW DEARS I WILL BE CHECKING UP ON YOU EVERY WOW AND AGAIN IF THAT'S OKAY AND I WANTED TO SAY THAT ANY PROBLEMS FROM BULLY'S TO PREGNANCY JUST COME TALK TO ME AND I WILL MAKE IT ALL BETTER OKAY WELL I WILL SEE YOU BOTH SOON" she then kissed them both and walked out shutting the door behind her leaving them both a little scared and even more worried

"Who the hell was that" he asked

"My aunt Julia... Yeah she's like that a lot" she laughed

"Really, is all your family like that" he asked

"Not really just her but I have no mother so-" she said

"Wait, what?" he interrupted

"oh, my mum died when I was a child and it always been me my dad and my brothers she just is like that to me as I'm the only other girl really left in the family" she answered

"Wow that's, I'm sorry" he said

"its okay I'm used to it that's why I didn't mind being with a guy for this because I knew that I don't really get along with girls and I'm used to guy's" she said

"Weird" he said

"How so" she asked

"well I still to this day don't know who my dad is and my mum has five other kid's all daughters I'm a lone boy in the family why I didn't mind sharing with a girl I just didn't think I get my female opposite" he said

"I know it's like they cloned us or something" she joked

"Yeah, no trying to eat me though please if you are a clone" he joked

"Same to you I guess" she said

they both laughed and continued unpacking when they were done the place seemed almost homely but not really welcoming Luna's desk had been taken up by her record player Isaac's by a DJ mix board but both still left space for work to be done most of the other shelves on both bookcases was taken up by more books, DVD's, video's , cd's and records the was now a large case next to Luna's bed she hadn't revealed what was in it and a similar case was under Isaac's bed but you wouldn't have noticed the main thing on his bed drawing the attention was a small moth eaten teddy bear sat against the pillow Luna didn't ask she didn't want to know really there was a small toy on Luna's bed a small turtle that sat on the pillow if she wasn't by the time everything was away they each just laid back on their bed's and sighed "that was hard work" he said

"I know right and we are not even done yet there is still stuff we need" she replied

"Lucky we have a week to get set before classes start" he

said

"Yep" she replied

Luna then got up and crossed the room and walked out to the balcony and looked across the road at the park it was sun set now it was setting just to the left of the balcony it was nice where they were the sun rose one side of the balcony went straight over head and set the other side there was only two floors above them but lot's below them for a while Luna just stood till she heard a loud crash and a scream from inside she ran back in to see Isaac stood on her bed arms in the air "what's the matter with you" she asked

"look" he said or more squeaked just pointing to under his bed she pulled up the bed sheet that had fallen on the floor where he had obviously dropped it she moved it and a large spider secured out she dropped the sheet screamed and joined Isaac standing on the other bed both now screaming and holding one to each other for what seemed like dear life till some guy walked in obviously annoyed at them both "what the hell are you screaming about in here" he said he was a tall man in gym clothes with huge muscles and a stern face obviously a sport's nut he just looked them both up and down and smirked "well what's with all the screaming" he said

"Spider" Isaac said or more squealed

"Really all this for some spider" he said

"You haven't seen it I swear to god it's a tarantula" Luna said

"Good I'm looking for one she got out her cage" he said

"What?" they both asked

He crawled along the ground for a second whistling till the spider came out from under the desk and crawled into his hand he then walked out Isaac and Luna didn't move from the bed or from the death grips they had on each other till he came back without the spider

"All good all taken care of relax... so are you to together?"

he said

"No why would you think that" Luna replied

"Well you have a pretty tight grip on each other" he said them both then releasing and letting go each other and backing away from both embarrassed and just fear they man laughed at them both "names Jake, Jake Newman" Jake said

"Isaac Richards"

"Luna Redgrave"

"So two people unisex room something going on" he asked

"No" they both snapped back

"Okay just asking is all I mean I'm next door with my girlfriend but you two are stranger's wow that's a bold move guy's" he said

"We keep getting told that" Isaac said

"Well if something does catch on I will be the one to say I called it first" he said

"Sure if you want" Isaac said in reply

"Cool" he then looked around the room "you guys have a lot of neat stuff in here but this seems like a lot are you guy's staying over semester breaks and stuff" he asked

"Well I am, I don't know about you?" Luna said turning to Isaac

"I don't know yet" Isaac answered

"Even though it still seems like a lot what set you guy's doing" he asked

"Twilight" Isaac said

"wow, you two are so going to hook up at some point I didn't even know they still ran the twilight set's but wow, just wow I'm on the moonlight set three year's but I can drop anywhere after the first and still pass , we'll chat later guy's" he said

He then turned and walked back out and shut the door they both then just sat on their own beds and calmed down after all that "what did he mean" Isaac asked

"Mean by what" she asked

"That we are 'sure to hook up at some point' " he said trying to mirror Jakes voice falling completely with his British sounding voice

"Well he assumes that two people who meet and share a room for such a long amount of time are bound to hook up" she answered

"Really I never thought about that" he said

"Relax I'm not interested Isaac" she reassured him

"Why not?" he asked sounding rather offended

"What?" she asked laughing slightly

"Well why not what's wrong with me" he asked again

"There's nothing wrong with you I'm just not the dating or hooking up type" she said

"You're not?" he asked

"No" she answered

"Good because neither am I" he said

"Really no way" she replied surprised

"Serious, you know something?" he asked

"What?" she asked

"I'm still a virgin" he said seriously

"No, I don't believe that Isaac I don't sorry" she laughed

"What about you?" he asked

"In every sense of the word still a virgin haven't even kissed a boy yet" she said

"No way. I don't think a girl like you could have never kissed a boy, I don't believe it" he laughed

"Believe what you want it's the truth" she said

"I haven't had my fist kiss yet either" he sighed

They both laughed for a moment before Luna got the courage to ask something we had wanted to ask all day

"can I ask you a personal question Isaac?"

"Sure" he said

"Are you gay?" she asked

"What?" he said sound offended again

"Really seriously are you?" she asked

"No, why would you think that?" he asked her

"sorry just it seemed to match up in my head that's all

the spider, all the fashion sense, the music and the good looks and the books and the movies it just sort of came of that way" she said

"Oh... So I'm good looking is I?" he said smugly

"What no...wait...that's not what I...uh...in some respects yes and in others no" she answered

"Thanks" he said smugly again

"Your welcome Isaac" she said falling backwards onto her bed

"well then Luna if we are begin honest your pretty but seem like a freak hiding behind a tough exterior that's how you came off to me" he said to her

"Cheer's" she laughed

"Your welcome Luna, so what we gunna do now" he asked

"What's the time?" she asked him

"About half six, you want dinner?" he said as he checked his watch

"Sure but no canteen food that stuff is meant to be awful" she replied

"Well the course stuff said we can leave when we want providing we are back before 11 so want dinner in town" he asked

"Sure, but how we gunna get there? Walk?" she joked

"No I can drive" he said

"Really" she asked

"Yes, I'm not completely useless just living of my good look's you know" he joked running a hand though his hair

"Shut up lets go before I eat you Isaac" she laughed

"Fine" he sighed

They both then locked up the room and headed out the grounds to the student car park Luna walked off expecting it to be a little mini or something but no it was a motorcycle pretty nice one too

"Well here she is the lady in my life" he said

"Wow she's Awesome Isaac" she answered

"I know, ever ride one of these before" he asked
"No" she replied
"Come on then let's go get some dinner I'm starving" he joked
"Okay" she said a bit worried
Luna then sat on the back behind leaving a extremely large gap between them Isaac then turned to look at her for a second "you really don't know what your doing do you" he laughed
"No I don't I don't even know where we are going" she said
"Come on" he laughed
he took her hands and wrapped them around him so she was safe and secure "okay you may what to hold on because I've never had a girl on her so I don't know quite how she's gunna react" and just in that second they were off driving at an amassing speed down the roads till they got into town and Isaac pulled in and parked in a small car park close to loads of fast food stores "so what do we want for dinner" he said
"I don't know" she answered
"What do you mean you don't know?" he asked
"I don't know you pick" she said
"Okay" he looked at all the places then made up his mind "I think going on the fact of our heritage by your voice I think fish and chips" he laughed sounding even more British then normal
"Good with me" she laughed
They then walked of and got dinner they sat for ages just talking more learning about each other till it started to get late "we should be getting back" Luna said
"Your right, let's just hope there won't be any more spiders in our room tonight" he said
"Yes that would be good" she laughed
by the time they finally left it was about half nine and they were both tired when they got back on his motorbike he said "now no yawning because if you fall

asleep I will fall asleep then we will crash and die got it no yawning" he said sternly
"Got it Isaac" she joked
she wrapped her hands around him again and as they went off a little steadier this time Isaac purposely ran over leaves to get them to fly in in the air and hit the street lamps or just fly up into the air in general after a few minutes Luna put her head on his shoulder and fell asleep Isaac just sighed and kept driving not before letting out a huge yawn of his own it had been a long day for both of them when they got back to the car park Isaac slowly moved his shoulder up and down till she woke up
"evening Luna" he said
"evening Isaac can I just have five more minutes" putting her head back and making sleep sounds "no come on you can sleep in a like ten seconds come on" he said
She eventually gave up and walked back to the room where they both almost immediately got into their beds and fell asleep.

Chapter 2

The first to wake was Isaac they had nothing to do today but he got up anyway he showered and was back dressed with only his hair still wet and on his laptop before Luna even got up "hey look who decided to get up this morning" he said smirking at her
"it's too early for you Isaac shut up" she said as she walked across the room and almost fell into the bathroom she had her shower and got dressed by the time that done Isaac still hadn't moved from his laptop
"We only have two towels" she said
"So?" he asked

"So we have now used both and have to do the washing" she said

"so?" he asked again

"soooo....stop sitting there with a towel wrapped round your shoulders, what are you doing any way you haven't moved since I got up" she asked

"Just looking" he said

"Looking at what" she asked

"Stuff" he said

"Helpful" she sighed

"Just trying to make a list up of what we need to buy desperately what can wait how we intend to get the stuff we need up twelve floors all that stuff" he answered

"well I know we need all matter of bathroom stuff, we need a fridge for sure possibly a hover we need kitchen stuff like bowls and plates and stuff we may need a table and a universal remove for the TV as this one doesn't have a remote" she added

"Good but how will we get a fridge from town to here with my bike and up here that's the real problem" he said

"True, we could ask to borrow my aunt's car for the day to transport stuff and get a hand from Jake or something to get it up here" she suggested

"Nice idea, I will go talk to Jake you can talk to our aunt" he said

"No, you talk to her I talk to him" she corrected

"What? , no way I'm not on my own" he said a bit scared

"Do you really want to go next door with the spider?" she asked

"You can talk to Jake, where's your aunt?" he asked

"She will be in the teachers block room 6" she answered

Isaac then went off to talk to Julia .When Isaac found the room he let out a sigh and prepared himself for the worst she opened the door in a tight pink and purple dress

"OH DARLING IT'S SO NICE TO SEE YOU" she said kissing him continuously all over his face "OH COME IN DEAR" she said opening the door more as he stepped in it revealed a large room about twice the size of theirs with all sorts of strange modern and colourful objects with a separate bedroom "NOW WHAT DID YOU WANT DEAR" she asked

"Oh...uh....Luna sent me to ask if we can borrow your car" he answered nervously

"MY CAR WHAT ON EARTH FOR DEAR" she asked

"Well we need some stuff and I only have a motorbike so we need a car and Luna said to ask you" he replied nervously

"OH WELL OF COURSE DEAR HERE" she handed him a pair of keys on a long chain with lots of little key rings on it she then almost pushed him out the door slamming it shut again behind him it seemed a tad out of character but he was just happy to be out of there and started walking back to the room all the way back he tried rubbing the lipstick of his face with no success anyone walking around just laughed at him hysterically.

meanwhile Luna went to talk to Jake next door she lightly taped on the door expecting to see Jake with a spider in his hand but instead it was a tiny sour faced girl with only half her make up done stood in a dressing down with her nails done but obviously from how she had her hands parted that they were still wet her hair was all tied up in rollers some of it blonde the rest red

"who the hell are you" she said in a high pitched American accent almost painful to hear

"I'm Luna from next door I was wondering if I could talk to Jake please" Luna asked

"Why love what you want to talk to him about?" the girl replied

"We have a problem that could use his assistance in" Luna said

the girl opened the door letting Luna lightly step in she girl walked in and sat on the bed drying her nails by blowing on them Jake was sat next to a spider tank tapping it lightly "hey Jake some girl here to see you" she said he picked his head up to see Luna "hey Lu what do you want, Isaac found another spider" Jake asked more like a joke

"No we want to know if you could do us a favour" Luna asked

"Sure what" Jake asked

"we are getting some stuff we need for the room some of which will be heavy we wanted to know if we can have some help with it latter to like move it around and stuff" Luna said

"Sure just give me a knock okay, oh have you met my wonderful girl here, angel say hi" he replied

"Hi" the girl said briefly

"She's next door with Isaac" he said to her

"Isaac that little nerd boy I feel sorry for you love if that's your man no wonder you look so pale girl" the girl said

"Oh no he's not-were not- we didn't come together we are just stranger's really" Luna said defencelessly

"Wow bold move honey well good luck with that one sweetie" the girl said

"thanks I guess, so I will ask for your help a little latter, thanks" Luna said before she walked out and back to the room where a little latter Isaac turned up with the key's and Julia's lipstick all over his face Luna tried not to laugh but it was difficult he looked ridiculous "don't you dare laugh at me Luna" he said looking very angry from being laughed at all the way back to the room but it was still funny "sorry Isaac I should have gone" she laughed

"It's okay I just-" he said trailing off

"Just what?" she asked

"This stuff won't come off today" he said rather annoyed

"Come with me I have a cure for this" she said

Luna then led him into the bathroom where she looked around the cuboid under the sink for a bit before pulling out a bottle of window cleaner

"What use is that?" he asked

"it's not lip stick Isaac it's lip ink much harder to get off

especially when dry, go and sit on you bed and I will fix
this" she replied
He then went off and sat up on his bed nervously waiting
"Okay Isaac just relax your face this may sting slightly
but try not to fig-git if I get this in your eye it's all over
okay" she said
"Okay" he answered
He shut his eyes as Luna removed his glasses and put
her glasses on
"Ready?" she asked
"Ready" he answered
she then put the small cloth on his head causing him
some slight stinging pain but as she began to rub the lip
ink of it was obvious it hurt he was moving and
complaining constantly about the pain he was in till
Luna had removed one part of the lip ink completely from
his face then placing a wet cloth to remove any of the
cleaner still on that part of his face "will you stop
complaining Isaac or do I have to put an apple in your
mouth?" she joked
"It hurts" he complained
"So don't complain about it" she said
"Don't help in not comfy" he complained again
"You're not meant to be comfy" she said
"Can't I grip something to stop me shouting" he asked
"fine" she looked around the room and till she found the
perfect object the old teddy bear on the pillow she picked
it up and gave it to him "here hug this thing" she said not
really wanting to touch it as she had no clue what it was
or where it had been
"Thing, I will have you know this is lord hugsly my bear
since birth and I would like you to respect him please" he
said
"Okay fine providing it shut's you up" she replied
she continued removing the lip ink from his face without
a sound from him he was like a little kid at times then
others like an adult it was like he couldn't quite find that

middle ground of his actual age he was either acting
older or younger but Luna didn't really ask questions she
guesses that he just enjoyed being like that she imagined
it must have been hard for him growing up without a dad
and surrounded by older sisters it was hard for her
growing up without a mother but it was rare she spoke
about it when she was done she gave him back his
glasses he looked strange without them his face seemed
really empty he was probably the only boy that looked
better with his glasses on then off he slowly put them
back on and opened his eye's still cuddling his teddy
bear
"Done?" he asked carefully
"Yes, you baby" she laughed
"Thanks" he said
"its okay I'm used to her I guess and it was my fault sort
of" she answered
"No it's fine at least we have the car now for the day" he
said
"I guess let's get going" she added
they both walked out to the car park Isaac followed Luna
as she knew what her aunt's car looked like when they
finally found it, they saw it was a small yellow mini
copper with a fabric interior that smelt of flowers they
started up the car and drove off into town to a
department store they got out the car and looked up at
this huge black building then walked inside the first
room was small with a huge notice on the wall and two
doors one said entrée the other exit the large notice had
what each floor contained written on it in huge block
capital's "uh start at the top and work down I guess"
Isaac said not a bad idea
"I think that would be the best idea" Luna replied
Isaac then walked off and got a large sort of luggage
trolley and they walked off into this huge store starting at
the top floor which was mainly lighting which they did
actually need as the main light for the room was just a

hanging light bulb and there was only one light in the bathroom "so we need a lamp" Luna said reading a list she had on her phone "what sort do you want" she asked him

"I don't mind a little one so we can still use the space on the table" he answered

"Well really bright or not that bright" she asked

"Don't mind" he answered

"Or do you just need a nigh light Isaac?" she joked

"no I don't need a night light but something to see if I need the bathroom I fell flat on my face this morning" he answered

"Okay fine what about that" she pointed so a small table light the bottom mimicked a brown pot sort of thing Isaac nodded and placed a boxed one in the bottom of the trolley lightly "what else" he said

"We need a better fitting for the main room light it's just hanging out the celling" she replied

"true it does sort of look like it's about to fall out the celling at me" he joked but the light sort of did look like that and they did say they could change what they wanted about the room "what about that one" he said pointing to one hanging from the ceiling on display it looked from below like a film real but it was a light a sort of chandelier that resembled film it was perfect for them this went on for around two hours just going around finding things by the time they had got everything they needed plus some stuff that just looked cool when they finally left and put everything in the car they went back to the room they did need Jakes help mainly for the large fridge freezer and the table everything else they could manage on their own by midday the room was full of boxes the fridge freezer fit perfectly into the space they had for it after putting a few bits and bob's away in specific places there was a knock at the door

"DARLINGS" the sighs of pain just by hearing that sound the horror they were gunna have to endure till Isaac got an idea "I've got it" he got the car keys and placed them on the bed then ran into the wardrobe "what are you doing?" she asked

"Hiding" he answered

"Not without me you're not" she said

Luna then ran into the wardrobe just beside him and they shut the door they tried to keep as quiet as possible while they heard her come in see walked in looked around sore the keys and put them in her hand bag unfortunately there was a spider in the wardrobe not a tarantula but a daddy long leg's only a few inches from Isaac's head he panicked but Luna put her hands over his mouth and kept him still so he didn't give them away she looked around some more then sighed and left as they heard her shut the door and walk away they both ran out the wardrobe terrified of the spider right to the pile of boxes

"Are you okay?" she asked

"I think so just terrified of both her and that spider" he answered

"Imagine her with a spider" Luna said

"Oh god the stuff of nightmares" he answered

"Come on let's get the rest of this stuff put away before it gets too late" she laughed

after putting a few of the things they bought in certain places around the room till they only had a few items left to put away one was the table another was a mirror to fit somewhere in the room and the light they then found a place to hang the mirror just by the door so if they went out somewhere they knew what they looked like when they got back they unpacked the table it was classic flat pack Isaac just sat on the floor looking at the instructions and the pieces and scratching his head in confusion looking more puzzled by the minuet till Luna sat down with him and took the instructions "well this is pretty simple" she said

"Really? Have you ever put a table together before?" he

asked
"Yes, why haven't you?" she asked
"No, I'm not good with wood I'm more electrics and cables and such" he answered
"Fine I can do this you watch and learn" she giggled
then in almost a few seconds the table was put together it was more like a bench no chairs they were built into it, it was like a park bench Isaac just sat back in shock looking at how fast she put that together he was in Aww of her for a moment till she slapped his head "hey Isaac pay attention" she said
"I was paying attention" he answered
"Okay what did I just say" she asked
"Uh...it's time for dinner" he said very unsure
"Lucky guess" she laughed
they both laughed before taking seat on the new table they bought food while they were out it was takeout food not really much more than chicken balls and chips really it wasn't very late the sun hadn't even set when they cleared away luckily they had bought a dish washer that day so no one was doomed with the horror of washing up.
"Okay what do we do now" he said
Luna just pointed up to the light falling out the celling
"Right, I will do that you just chill do what you want till I'm done okay" he said
"Okay" she replied
Luna sat on her bed she had her shower earlier so she just sat in a small black vest top and her jeans on her bed with her laptop just in front of her on the bed so she could sit up and use it, Isaac stood on a small step he borrowed from Jake so he could reach the celling to fix the light he took his jacket and over shirt of so he stood with just a white t-shirt and his jeans and started working his eye's fixed on the celling looking at cables and electric shockers for a second Luna looked up at him she could see straight up his shirt from that angle he

was thin he looked attractive almost muscular under his shirt he then stood up slightly revealing the waist band of his boxers over his jeans before Luna quickly returned her eye's to the laptop screen a few seconds later Isaac looked down to get a screwdriver before noticing he could see most of the top of her shirt from that high he prayed she couldn't see him looking at her as her glasses where mirroring the screen he almost didn't what to stare but found it difficult till he moved a cable wrong and gave himself a small electric shock from not really paying attention then returned his gaze to the light fixture again even if he did try a few more quick glances but so did she till one try he made to move slightly just as he was finishing of as she moved her gaze back to him catching them both out she at least lessened the silence with a joke "eye's front mister"

"oh-sorry I did-I didn't realise that uh..." he trailed of really not thinking what to say went he finished the light and turned it in it fitted the room nicely "now take that step back your lethal with it" she said to him with a laugh he returned the step angel giving him a strange look when he did he wasn't sure if she was angry, upset or something else but he just walked back to the room he sat on his bed for a bit without saying much looking at the case next to Luna's bed "hey Luna" he said

"Hey Isaac, what do you want?" she asked

"What's in that case?" he asked

She turned her head to see it

"Oh you mean my baby" she said

"You're what?" he asked

she got up putting her laptop to the floor making all her bed clear she gently put the case of the bed and opened it revealing a black and white bass guitar "wow that's a nice baby" he said

"Thank you" she replied

Isaac then got the case from under his bed it contained a red and black electric guitar

"Wow, that's beautiful Isaac" she said
"Thanks" he answered
They sat on the others bed picking up the other's guitar and examining it in their hands
"Nice neck length, good stings, all in tune nice your baby got a name" he said
"Danny" she answered
"Really?" he asked
"Yeah why" she asked
"Nothing just a strange name that all any real reason behind that or what" he asked
"A bitter sweet story I guess" she answered
"Oh sorry I shouldn't have-" he said
"it's okay it's the best story I know, when I was younger I knew a man called Danny he was a wonderful man taught me everything I know really more than my dad he hasn't been the same since mum died he really became my dad and something happened to him I never sore him again I know where he is he knowns where I am but we don't talk about what happened, it's just not something we talk about" she said
"Wow, I didn't know you were so deep sometimes" he joked
"there's a lot you don't know about me Isaac" she said he didn't know how to take that it seemed sad but happy it was stage but the conversation quickly moved along "it's a nice bass I'm not gunna lie" he said
"Well what would know about bass guitars?" she asked
He gave her a look then began playing a quick tune on it he played really well he must have done it before
"Nice" she said when he had finished "well yours is in a good shape, nice range on it over all nice does your baby have a name?" she asked
"Melody" he answered
"Really" she asked
"Yeah" he answered
"Any reason for that or-" she said

"My sister, my only younger sister she ran off we still don't know where" he interrupted

"Sorry" she said

"It's okay, I guess we have both had hard life's" he joked

"Yeah" she sighed

"But what do you know about guitars?" he asked

She then shot him a similar look and started playing and singing

Twenty flight rock extremely well Isaac just sat there mouth open gazing at her till she finished "wow, you didn't say you could sing" he said a bit surprised

"I never said I couldn't did I can you?" she asked

He just shrugged "come on just a few words' Isaac" she asked

"No I refuse to sing while sober" he answered

they both laughed putting the guitars back into the right cases and back to their original places then they both sat on the ends of their bed's watching some tv till they heard shouting they muted the tv it was coming from next door it was Jake and angel they were fighting over something they couldn't think what till they heard loud and clear "LOOK ANGEL I'M YOU BOYFRIEND YOU CAN JUST SLEEP WITH ANY GUY THAT COMES KNOCKING AT THE DOOR" clearly Jake said

"WHY NOT LIKE YOU WOULDN'T DO IT TOO WHILE YOUR OFF WITH YOUR SPORT'S GUYS AT SOME BAR I'M STUCK HERE IN THIS LITTLE ROOM WHAT AM I MEANT TO DO WITH MY TIME" angel replied

"I DON'T KNOW FIND A HOBBY OR HERE'S AN IDEA ANGEL WHYDON'T YOU GET A JOB" Jake suggested

"HOW DARE YOU INSULT ME LIKE THAT" she replied

"NO REALLY ANGEL HOW ABOUT YOU GET A JOB I'M TIRED OF TRYING TO KEEP UP WITH YOUR SPENDING I HAVE WORK TO DO NOW I CANT BE SPORTING YOU TWO"

"ALL I SPEND IS IMPORTANT"

"YES ESSENTIAL TO LOOKING LIKE A TART" then a

door slam and some more inaudible shouting till they heard a knock at the door they opened it, it was Jake standing there almost crying

"Hey guy's you heard all that then" he said
"We only heard what you want us to hear" Isaac said "It's okay, I wanted to ask can I-" he asked
"Yes" Luna said
"What you don't even know what I was gunna-" he said
"You want to ask if you can stay here for a while till this blows over. Sure it's fine come in" Luna said interrupting him again
He stepped in the room then looked around obviously admiring the changes already made in the room "wow, nice place guy's" he said
"We wanted it to be a bit more like home" Isaac said
After a few minutes of showing off some of the stuff he asked about Isaac asked the burning question in everyone's mind "so where do you want to sleep?"
"Uh I don't really mind" Jake answered
"Well you could share my bed if you want" Isaac added
"If its okay I sleep alone man I know your good intentions but I don't really know you" Jake said
"True, how about you take my bed I will have the floor" Isaac suggested
"Oh for god sake, Jake take Isaac's bed, Isaac can take mine" Luna interrupted
"Where are you gunna sleep?" Jake asked
"I don't really sleep at night anyway, it's okay I will sit up and sleep tomorrow"
"No way either you have your bed and I take the floor or I share with Jake your sleeping either way" Isaac said
"Why don't you two just share" Jake said not really trying to imply anything just giving an idea after a few moments of thought Isaac said
"I'm okay with that"
"You know I'm in no frame of mind to argue, fine" Luna

replied

After a few minutes Jake

Claimed into Isaac's bed and Isaac into Luna's with his teddy bear Luna stood out on the balcony till she was sure they were asleep before getting into the other side of her bed far from Isaac it was beyond weird now they meet less than a week ago now they were sharing a bed it was just plain strange after a few hours of restless sleep Luna woke up Jake was awake to but it was about midnight he was stood on the balcony smoking she walked up to the door he looked like he was crying "you okay Jake" she asked

"Oh hey Lu shouldn't you be asleep" he asked

"I told you I don't really sleep at night and it's even harder to sleep knowing he's at the other end of the bed" she answered

"what's with you two, one second I could swear you two are in love other's you hate each other which is it" he asked

"I don't know, give me one of them will you" she said he then gave her one and she look so relieved after the first smoke as she blew out the smoke into the dark of the night sky

"You're a bundle of surprises Lu" he laughed

"Thanks, so what is up with you and angel" she asked

"Nothing it will blow over I'm sure" he said

"Okay" she replied

"But what about you?" he asked

"What do you mean?" she asked

"What do you or do you not see in Isaac" he asked

"I told you I don't know" she laughed

"No you know I can see it in your eye's you know, come on lu" he said

"I don't know he's like a little kid sometimes, hugging his teddy bear and screaming about spiders then there's other times like when he rides his motorbike and when he's gaming good moments he seems really grown up, but he's broken" she said

"Aren't we all" he joked

"No I really mean it Jake he is broken" she said

"But come on Luna little bit of care can fix anything" he replied

"Not everything" she said sadly

"What do you mean" he asked

"There's a lot he doesn't know about me stuff he can't know about me, I don't what to put him in any danger not now, it's hard to fix a broken person when you're smashed beyond repair" she said

"Sorry I shouldn't have asked" he said

"It's fine I just don't what him to get into anything he can get out of easily" she said

"That's what you mean, you want to love him but you know you can't let him love you" he said

"Exactly" she replied

"What's going on out here" a voice said from the door it was Isaac rubbing his eyes under his glasses and yawning obviously just woke up.

Chapter 3

"Nothing Isaac just chatting that's all" Jake said turning to him

"Luna, are you smoking?" Isaac asked

"Yes Isaac, why?" she asked

Isaac then walked up to the pole next to Luna he took the cigarette out her hand and smoked it himself before handing it back for her to do the same this process continued for a few goes Jake just laughed at them both

"what" Luna asked

"You two are so cute and you don't even realise, it's great" Jake laughed

at that moment they saw angel walking out the building Jake looked like he was gunna cry again before Luna spat down and hit her causing both boy's to laugh at her before Jake did the same and Isaac followed suit before long they were all spiting at her from the balcony sat she walked off into the distance they all laughed

"Thanks guy's I don't know what I would do without you" Jake said

"your welcome any time mate" Isaac said passing the cigarette to Luna after that Jake went back to his own room leaving Luna and Isaac still awake looking out still sharing the cigarette's watching as the sun come up till Isaac broke the long running silence "what did he mean"

"Mean by what Isaac" she asked

"You know exactly what Luna, do you know how long I was stood there behind you before I spoke up" he said

"No why hear something important" she said trying to ignore him a bit

"You could say that" he sighed

"Well what did you hear if you don't mind me asking" she asked

"Just something" he sighed

"What, just spit it out Isaac" she said a bit annoyed

"You can't fix a broken person when you're smashed beyond repair" he said repeating what she had said earlier

"Good advice Isaac" she said

"We are both broken but you're not smashed yet a while" he said

"You don't know that" she sighed

"yes I do I can see it in your face Luna even if you are smashed I can fix smashed things just got to get out the super glue that's all, come on Luna we have five years together we might as well try to fix our broken brains" he suggested Luna didn't say anything for a while not till the sun hung quite high in the sky "fine, I'm not in a position to argue with you Isaac" she said not sounding all too happy about it

"Okay, so what we gunna do today" he asked

"I don't know game, shop, home improves, I don't know" he sighed
"What about you, me, the bike and all the time in the world" he suggested
"Where are we gunna go?" she asked
"I don't know" he said
"When will we get back?" she asked
"I don't know" he said again
"What will we do?" he asked
"I don't care" he said

"Okay" she sighed

they both got dressed and went off to the car park there was a lot more people arriving today the shorter causes students were arriving now but they just walked by them all getting a few strange looks from a few girls and a few boy's they were not sure why till they got on the motorbike getting a few wolf whistles from the boy's and a couple of angry glares at Luna from the girls obviously jealousy, till she heard one say "I guess you want the hot ones you got to get here early" just making them both laugh and dive of into the road the roads where all covered in leaves they had no clue where they were going they drove straight through town and off into just fields no houses just fields surrounding the road stretching for miles they just kept driving though no matter what passed them they just kept driving almost continuously till they passed over a hill and they saw a large city they went sure what city it was they were both unfamiliar with the place they were having both come from England after all they found a car park and they stopped "where are we Isaac?" she asked
"I don't know but I guess we can find out, come on" he said
she looked very worried but so did he it was like being intentionally lost somewhere the place was huge with

skyscrapers everywhere and billboards covering every surface it was a good place provided you didn't look down if you looked down you could see the rubbish, the rats ,the homeless and the drug addicts everywhere and the place seemed like a living hell hole it was strange that something this bad could be so close to what they had come from every sound and thing scared them both like children lost without their parents till it started to rain first lightly then heavily all the people but Isaac and Luna ran inside even the rat's "why don't we go inside my glasses are fogging up I can't see thing" Isaac said
He wasn't lying he couldn't see a thing he may have been talking to a wall for all he knew

"Come on Isaac I love the rain and there's no one else around now" she said
"But I can't see where I'm going Luna" he complained
"come here" she said as she took his hand from his pocket and griped it tightly to at least give him a scene of direction he used his other hand to clean his glasses so he could sort of see a bit they walked around for a while till a car went speeding past drenching them both in water

 "I vote back to the bike" Isaac said
"Me to" Luna replied spiting the water out her mouth they both then ran hand in hand back to the bike and drove of back towards WestBrook the closer they got the nicer it got the rain stopped the sun shone and it just seemed like such a nicer atmosphere then the other place when they got back everyone was about on the grass talking and other stuff most people around turned to look at them it was quite strange they went off in the early hours of the day together and came back covered in water huddled together Jake saw them and came running up to them "what the hell happened to you guy's" he asked

"I think we found hell" Isaac said
"Really, well there is someone in your room to see you two." Jake replied
"Who?" Luna asked
"I think you will know when you see them" Jake said they both walked slowly back to their room hesitating before opening the door they noticed a woman in a black dress with her nose in the air as Isaac sore her he turned as white as a sheep "m-m-m-mum w-w-w-what are you d-d-d-doing here?" he said his stutter was back like when Luna first met him it was strange more like the stutter was a thing he did around his family or something she simply looked at him and frowned "over a week Isaac, over a week and no sigh of you anywhere it thought you had ran off like Melody, luckily my idea was right you came here early but you're not staying here young man pack you things we are leaving" she said
"What the hell do you mean I'm not going anywhere" he answered
"DON'T YOU DARE SWEAR AT ME NOW I AM YOUR MOTHER AND I SAY WE ARE GOING HOME, all this foolish collage business you are going home to get a real job, a steady wife and a family of your own your life Isaac are you going to throw it away on a hunch" she shouted
"I-I-I-I-I-it's not a hunch mum I can do this" he stuttered
"No you can't Isaac we are going-who's this" she said just noticing Luna
"l-l-l-Luna redg-g-g-grave" he stuttered
"Hi" Luna said quietly
"What's this a little friend already I told you Isaac you are to be married to Melissa Harding next year" she said rather annoyed
"no I'm not mum you can tell me what I'm going to do or what I'm not" Isaac said almost shouting now he didn't look angry just upset it was obvious his mother wanted to control him and he had obviously ran of

"yes I can I am your mother, and guess what your grounded when we get home don't think I can't smell it in here you've been smoking again haven't you, all this a week and what do I find my boy gone off on some silly collage course, I come to get him to find he has found some little tart ,been smoking, probably drinking too and answering back to his own mother clearly you need less time out of the house Isaac, now I will be waiting down stairs I expect you to be down in an hour with all your things ready to give up this stupid idea and come home to the plan set out for you Melissa is destroyed her FUTURE husband was missing. now please Isaac get started" she said sourly before   then left shutting the door behind her Isaac just fell on his bed with his head in his pillow crying his eye's out "oh Isaac" Luna said sitting next to him pulling him up and hugging him "it's okay, you don't have to do anything she say's"
"Yes I do she's my mum I don't have a choice Luna" he answered
"Well why not, she may be your mother but you're not a child anyone this is your choice to stay here." she replied
"I know I want to stay here but she will just get worse she won't leave without me" he complained
"Then she will have to wait five years for you then" Luna said cheering him up a bit "who's Melissa?" she asked
"What?" he asked
"Who is she?   I'm just curious is all" she said
"Some friend of the family my mum likes I don't in fact I hate her but we are engaged to be engaged to be engaged by our parents" he sighed
"Wow, she can't just do that" Luna said
"That's my mum" he sighed
"You know what" Luna giggled
"What?" he asked
"All those plans your mother has for you will wait" Luna said
"Your right I'm gunna walk down and tell her" he said

getting up and standing like he was going to leave but
not moving
"Don't bother" Luna said
"What why not" he asked sitting down again rather
happy to not go down and face his mother
"Make her come ask you why you're not going anywhere"
Luna said
"You are the best person I have ever met Luna" he said
"Same" she laughed
about an hour passed of just doing what they would
normally do sitting on their laptops, watching TV and
listening to music till around and hour and a half later
she was back storming in her face red with anger "what
are you doing Isaac" she asked
"Playing games mum why?" he answered being now sat
on the end of his bed playing game on his console
without even removing his glare from the screen
"You should be packing to go home Isaac" she said sourly
"No I don't think so mum" he answered
"What?" she asked angrily
"I'm not going anywhere" he said
"I beg your pardon" she said sourly
"I'm not going anywhere mum you're going home I will be
home when my course is finished maybe if I don't have
other plans" he said
"No your coming home to live your life Isaac" she replied
sourly
"No I'm staying here to live my own life" he replied
"No I'm your mother you will do as you're told" she said
trying to keep some control over him
"That may have worked back then but not now mummy I
will call you in half term okay" he then pushed her out
the door and slammed it locking it up before re-entering
the room looking extremely happy
"You feel better now" Luna asked
"Defiantly" he answered
after a few minutes they when outside for a shared

cigarette when they sore his mother storm across the path giving them both one last glare before leaving as the sun set it was a nice night so nice they moved the table out onto the balcony and ate outside in the twilight after dinner they moved the table back to stand looking at the stars while SHARING another cigarette they went sure why they all way's shared them it was just a fun thing to do they stood ,smoked and chatted "thank you Luna, I think if it wasn't for you I would be home by now" he said
"No need Isaac you would have done it yourself I know you" she replied
"Liar" he joked shoving her slightly
"Exactly" she laughed
They both stood silently for a moment enjoying the twilight
"Why would she have made all those plans for you how long has she been like that" Luna asked
"As long as I can remember always had a plan for me" he said
"Which is?" she asked
"as I remember it, get perfect grades though primary school, go to the best secondary my family could find, go to a high standing British collage then to Oxford university, marry Melissa Harding ,have six kid's, a house in London and a house in Blackpool, with a job as a professor at some university" he answered
"Wow, that's some plan hope you don't mind but what went wrong" he asked
"I failed most of my a levels except media and drama then when my mum was out I applied here I had saved all my money for years got on a plane that would take my bike and came here and met you" he said
"Wow sounds like quite a life Isaac" she joked
"Thanks but after this me and Melody off somewhere god knows where and pay my bills with my guitar" he said
"Nice Isaac real nice" she said
"What about you?" he asked

"How so?" she asked in reply

"Do you have a plan, even just a brief one?" he asked

"No I'm more surviving day to day then big epic planning" she answered

"What you gunna do when we leave?" he asked

"I don't know, who known's maybe in five years I will have a plan" she joked

"You know if you want, I could always use a bassist" he said seriously

"No thanks Isaac I travel alone" she said

"Why?" he asked

"it's just-" she began

"safer, you said that last night look I know it's probably none of my business but how is it safer, safer from what" he asked

"Nothing just... nothing Isaac, come on let's get some sleep" she said

Luna then walked back into the room leaving Isaac worriedly stood on the balcony they both went then to bed put Isaac just lay looking at her in her bed worrying not knowing what she meant till around 1:00 am he got up and went to talk to Jake he knocked on the door and a few moment's latter Jake opened it looking extremely tired

"Hey Isaac what's up man" Jake said sound as tired as he looked

"Something I really need to talk to you about" Isaac said franticly

"Sure shoot man" Jake replied

"Can I explain in there" Isaac asked

"Sure I guess" Jake sighed

They both then went into Jake's room he sat on the bed and Isaac stood passing rapidly but keeping quiet

"something has been turning in my head all day and I think I need help" Isaac said

"Help with what Isaac" Jake asked

"Luna" Isaac said in a hushed whisper

"What about her?" Jake asked

"Last night I heard the two of you talking about some stuff I can't stop thinking about it" Isaac answered

"About what exactly Isaac?" Jake asked

"About like stuff I can't know, to put me in danger and today she said that she travels alone because it's safer" Isaac said

"I see your point Isaac but that's not much you know she could just be an UN sociable person" Jake yawned

"No Jake it's more than that, I know it is something deeper something strange about her I just- I just can't escape the feeling something up" Isaac replied

"Oh I know what this is your in love with her already, I called it man" Jake said laughing slightly and quietly

"No, I'm not in love with her Jake" Isaac snapped

"Yes you are you like totally are man" Jake said sounding pleased with himself

"No I'm not because I found something today I haven't told her about yet" Isaac said

"What did you find out?" Jake asked

"Luna Redgrave is legally dead" Isaac answered

"What?" Jake asked in shock

"Luna Redgrave only daughter of the Redgrave family, ran off when she was nine years old from the family home missing ever since now confirmed legally dead, don't you think I would have Goggled the girl my room-mate while I have been here" Isaac explained

"What the hell" Jake asked

"My thought's exactly when I read it" Isaac said

"Then who the hell is that in your room?" Jake asked

"I don't know I intend to talk to her about what I know" Isaac answered looking quiet confused

"DON'T" Jake said

"What?" Isaac asked

"don't talk to her see if she gets used to you and tells you on her own, that's got to be better than asking her she's more likely to panic if you ask her" Jake explained

"Your right but what am I meant to do?" Isaac asked
"Just be patient Isaac, drop a few maybe hints or
questions now and then to try and make her tell you
without noticing" Jake suggested
"Okay, thanks Jake" Isaac replied
"Your welcome man but I stand by what I said" Jake said
"What do you stand by?" Isaac asked

"I stand by your in love with her Luna Redgrave or not
you like her no denying that Isaac" Jake said
"shut up Jake" Isaac said before leaving and returning to
the room where he sore Luna was already awake
standing in her pyjama's looking out the door at the rain
on the balcony she looked happy but she didn't turn to
see him

 "Hey" he said
"Hey" she replied
"You okay?" he asked
"Yeah just worried I think" she answered
"What about?" he asked standing beside her?
"Well we start work tomorrow just nerves I guess" she
answered
"Don't worry we'll be fine I'm sure" he said shoving her
arm slightly

"Yeah" she said

"Yeah, what do we have anyway I don't know my
timetable" he asked
"Drama on Monday, media on Tuesday, core English on
Wednesday morning, core maths Wednesday afternoon,
media on Thursday and drama on Friday" she answered
"Wow lots of stuff then hope we get the same classes" he
said
"I hope so do but we are on the same room's so we
should be" she said more like a joke as it was funny he

couldn't remember

"Course I forgot, just be being stupid again" he laughed

"When are you not Isaac" she laughed in reply

they both laughed in that moment Isaac almost completely forgot the conversation he just had with Jake maybe he was right maybe he did think about her a bit too much but if so it couldn't be helped

"Who's our teacher for drama" he asked

"Uh, a mister...dentrodelteatro he sound's delightful" she said

Chapter 4

after the day went by with them both not doing much it came as hell to wake up at the alarm six in the morning they both woke up annoyed and tired after taking turns for the shower and getting dressed Luna wore like normal jeans and black shirt with a small jacket over the top Isaac just had his jeans and the classic two shirt thing going on, they then went off to find the theatre it was relatively simple to find it was a large room with lights everywhere and two main blocks of seats the hole room was black there was not many people when they first arrived but lots more soon after they sat next to each other in one of the main seat blocks putting their books on their lap's till the seat's where full and a man entered from the stage door on the left "morning student's" he said in a strange accent he was quiet a large man quite fat and not very muscular he had long brown hair tied at the back into a ponytail he had a pink top on and tight brown trousers he looked at everyone then frowned before continuing to talk

"now I expect most of you hear are thinking oh drama all messing around quoting Shakespeare lines and playing hooky but NO NOT IN MY CLASS here you will learn to act perfectly and flawlessly AND YOU WILL BE

FLAWLESS WHEN I'M DONE WITH YOU now the first thing we do is the production all will be given parts in a play I wrote, a musical all will do this as it is imperative to your final grade at the end of the semester now all of you out here boys on the left girls on the right" everyone filleted out into two crowds both Luna and Isaac staying way to the back trying not to be seen by him he told the boy's to return to their seats and they all did so to let the girls spread out into a long line Luna and Isaac could see each other they were slightly smirking as he walked past several girls not even giving them a glance before getting to the centre and stepping out as to see them all "girls raise your hand if you can't sing" many girls not including Luna raised their hands and he told them to sit back down there was only about ten of them now "girls please sing for me from anything" he started at one end of the line far from Luna calling a last name then waiting for a line each was quiet simple Luna looked at Isaac nervously, he mouthed to her to sing twenty flight rock as the names got closer she began to panic but as soon as she heard it "Redgrave" she sang a line perfectly stretching out some of the notes of twenty flight rock the others had been quite quiet but Luna's voice echoed though the theatre getting a few looks from other girls and a few boy's "perfect" he shouted "your my perfect Isabella with that voice" he then gave her a script she was a main part other girls then had to go back and do more things but Luna just sat reading with Isaac he was just being nosy as to what this was about having no success when all the girls had parts small or otherwise he called up the boy's they all stood in a long line with Isaac in a similar place to where Luna was he was looking extremely nervous after all the stuff girls had to do he was a bit worried Mr dentrodelteatro walked around for a moment just looking at the boy's before shouting almost screaming "NO, NO GOOD boy's jackets off" and all the boy's with slight hesitation took of their jackets and put them on the floor he then walked around again his face turned red with anger he pointed a few boy's to sit down for a bit then a few more than a few more than a few more till five boy's remained Isaac inculcated he seemed a bit out of place though the others where all quite tall muscular boy's all good looking and strong then right in the middle was little skinny and lanky Isaac with his glasses it got to the last four of them before he said anything else to them "OKAY BOY'S SHIRTS GROUND NOW PLEASE" all of them looked stunned and a bit confused what was he asking them to do till he repeated even louder than before "boy's shirts off please" all of them looked at the girls Isaac's eye's fixed on Luna he was looking terrified the other three boy's took of their shirts without hesitation obviously wanting to impress the girls in the room but Isaac was not quiet to eager he took of his over shirt and put it on the floor but stood for a second looking at all the girls in the room before Mr dentrodelteatro shouted directly at him "MR RICHARDS BOTH SHIRTS PLEASE" with a lot of shaking and regret he took of his other shirt revealing much more than Luna sore when he was fixing the light she was almost smirking at him now before he crosses his arms over his now bare chest getting a couple of wolf whistles from the sitting boy's UN like the other boy's Isaac wasn't covered in muscle he looked almost anorexic just breathing made the lower half of his rib cage obvious all the other boy's also had a lot of body hair whereas Isaac had none what so ever it was almost funny how out of place he looked, Mr dentrodelteatro walked passed them all looking intently at all four of them before telling two to sit down again leave now just Isaac and a rather muscular man with the   name of Harrison, unfortunately for Isaac all the girls had their eye's fixed on Harrison making Isaac feel extremely UN-comfortable begin next to him till he spoke again after a long contemplation "right Harrison your my Jacob, Richards

your my Aron" he gave them both a different script then told them to sit back down and the other boy's to get up Isaac quickly picked up his shirts and put them back on while Harrison just sat around about twelve girls with his shirt in his hand Isaac sat back with Luna looking at the character list in the front of the script looking at who the people given parts where in the musical before long they started to whisper to each other at the back of the hall
"who are we again" Isaac said
"I'm Isabella and your Aron" she answered
"What does it say?" he asked
"It say's I'm a shop clerk, with a echoing voice and no interest in the common practice of the town" she answered
"What common practice?" he asked
"Courting" she said
"What about me?" he asked
"it say's Aron is Jacobs brother with more brain the brawn, but a habit of staying locked away for hours on end while his brother converses with young maidens" she answered
"Really?" he asked
"Yep" she said
"This is gunna be fun I can tell" he said sarcastically
After a few seconds of the other boy's getting parts he called for everyone to come sit on the stage in a circle just with their scripts and they would begin a read of the first main dialogue of the first scene between Aron and Jacob
"okay boy's for now just read your lines no voices or acting just yet this is a brotherly conversation" he then began ready the stage directions and when either Isaac or Harrison spoke they were reading from the script in front of them that when as follows:
The day opens with a bird song and a bright light from the door enters Jacob to see his brother Aron sat on his bed deep in though

J:"oh now I say dear brother what is wrong?"
*A:"nothing much just thought and dream crossing paths
once more Jacob"*
*J:"really Aron you really must listen people of the town
will think you odd staying inside thinking during courting
season, shame sir shame"*
*A;"UN like by brawn filled brother I do not care much for
courting young maidens"*
*J:"and why not dear brother it is a wonderful game or
perhaps you have your eye on some young lady here
about"*
A:"no all seem like maidens no lady's here"
*J:"really what though that little shop clerk you see almost
all days of the week is not she a lady"*
A:"I don't know Jacob"
*J:"I swear sir she is a lady still, no man has ever courted
her before she's impossible"*
A:"maybe I will break that law of impossibility
*J:"you won't get two steps of the courting chain Aron all
have tried and failed"*
*A:"well since I don't know the chain it would be UN fair to
say so Jacob"*
J:"you know the steps you see them everyday"
*A:"true but I bet my life savings I would make it at least
three by the end of the season"*
J:"I bet you won't"
A:"shall we then"
They then shake hands making there bet official before
Jacob is of out again to see some young maiden
"so gentleman that really set's the scene for the whole
performance as this scene really make the production
focus on the topic which is of course a town in the mist
of courting season and two almost refusing to court
setting out on the impossible challenge now scene two
across the street girls" the teacher said
The next scene followed like this:
Open to a small shop with two young clerk girls Isabella

and Maria talking casually as Maria is about to leave

M:"dear girl you work too hard"

I:"no Maria I work just hard enough maybe you should spend less time courting and more time working"

M:"oh but no dear Isabella courting is so much fun how do you sit back year after year the boys have begun to call you impossible"

I:"oh but I am not impossible I just have my standards Maria, I won't court for the sake of it I want to be courted for love not for fun"

M:"dear you are impossible or do you lie in wait for your special man to come a courting you"

I:"perhaps"

M:"oh do tell Isabella"

I:"no I won't tell a soul I swear on my life I won't tell a soul"

M:"I bet I can guess"

I:"I bet you can't Maria"

M:"okay.... the watchmakers son"

I:"no"

M:".....the farmer's son"

I:"no"

M:"the ink keeper's eldest boy... the garden boy... the butcher, the baker, the candlestick maker"

I:"no, no, no, no and no"

M:"oh do tell Isabella I promise I won't tell"

I:"you really want to know"

M:"yes I'm dying to know Isabella"

I:"fine... the book makers son"

M:"which one? "

I:"you know perfectly well which one Maria"

M:"oh not the show of one the little one"

I:"yes all right Aron"

M:"oh... Isabella, he's a weird one he doesn't even court"

I:"I know that"

M:"oh look here come's your boy now"

Maria then runs out the door leaving Isabella alone

shaking her head as Aron enters

"And we will continue next time thank you gentlemen, ladies" Mr Dentrodelteatro said letting everyone pack up there things and return to their rooms when Isaac and Luna returned they sat down on their beds and sighed

"Well that was certainly eventful" Luna said

"How so?" he asked

"Well we know what we are doing for the rest of the semester and I got to see most boys with their tops off" she laughed

"Oh god that was horrible I am never doing that again" he sighed

"Oh shut up Isaac it wasn't that bad" she giggled

"It was awful having to stand next to that man candy" he said

Luna laughed at him "what's so funny?" he asked

"Does it ever occur to you the girls where looking at you not him" she said

"You don't have to nice to me Luna, I am aware most girls in there cringed at me when I took my shirt off" he sighed

"No they didn't Isaac most girls I could see where impressed" she said

"Really?" he asked getting all existed

"Yes you should heard them Isaac they loved you a couple where actually interested" she said

"Nice, I guess" he sighed

"Okay but new room rule" she said

"What?" he asked

"If you get a girl in here you text me or make a sign so I know" she said

"Relax the only girl I let in here is you and your aunt...with a fight" he said

"Okay give that a few weeks it will be a different one every day" she laughed

"No way I'm not like that Luna my rule no girls expect you are allowed in here" he said

"aww thanks Isaac that make me feel so much better"
she said sarcastically after a few minutes they had
dinner it was a long first day with certain embarrassment
for the both of them. The next few days and weeks
continued much like before just getting up going to class
returning back to the room and discussing things of little
importance the productions was still in early stages they
were focusing on the main large parts of dialogue
between character's in the first few scenes of the first act
,one Friday night they were given work and told to read
though properly act 1 scene 3 one they hadn't previously
read Isaac sat on his bed with his leg's crossed and his
script in his lap Luna laid on her bed facing down with
her script in front of her and they attempt to read
thought the laughable scene:

A:"oh good morning dear Isabella"
I:"morning Aron to what end do I see you today"
A:"no end Isabella just simple chat is all I seek"
I:"many have tried that Aron"
A:"tried what"
I:"the simple chat line I believe six try to be different Aron"
A:"dam"
I:"are you actually trying dear Aron"
A:"perhaps I am"
I:"you should know not to bother, anyone known's I'm
impossible especial for a first try at courting"
A; "perhaps I'm not courting exactly"
I:"then what are you doing"
"Luna?" Isaac said
"Isaac you broke the scene" Luna replied
"Sorry, a stage direction three line's down" he said
Luna looked at the stage direction it was a difficult stage
direction to read without laughing as they now knew
Isaac was going to have to kiss her
"Oh god" Luna said laughing hysterical
"I think we will have to talk to him, explain the situation

we can't do that"
Luna looked though to other pages that they were on "Isaac you may want to turn to act 3 page 7" and he did there was a lot more romantic infatuation between the characters of Aron and Isabella thought the performance this was gunna be difficult.

Chapter 5

when they returned on Monday morning they were meant to be blocking out the scene on the stage with the scripts begin told what to do while reading it they both stood on the stage smirking completely aware of what was to come and very terrified as each second went by Mr dentrodelteatro would be shouting an order at a person in the scene with Isabella and Maria till Isaac new he had to enter all the lines where said perfectly but in audible from he shouts of Mr dentrodelteatro as Isaac first entered it was "LOOK INTERESTED IN THE CHARACTER MR RICHARDS" it was difficult for them to try to keep straight faces while being given the orders but Luna wasn't getting many it was mainly Isaac as it went on like they had read it before he kept getting more orders of where to go and where to stand how to look
"MR RICHARDS GET CLOSER TO LUNA PLEASE" it was now that they were saying there line's with in and few inches of each other Luna could tell how nervous Isaac was by the rate he was breathing almost hyperventilating till it got to the stage direction they had both been loathing Isaac new it was there and began to stumble on that final line just before it then just plainly looking at Luna appositely petrified till he got another order
"ISAAC PLEASE JUST KISS THE GIRL" he teacher shouted
"Can I talk to you about that" Isaac asked

"I GUESS GO ON" the teacher sighed

"Can I not do that" he asked

"IF YOU DON'T DO THIS YOU WILL FAIL THIS FOR THE ENTIRE SEMESTER MR RICHARDS" the teacher answered

"Is there any way I can get out of this kissing stuff without failing" he asked

"NO IT'S ESSENTIAL TO THE PERFORMANCE, NOW PLEASE FROM LINE 16" the teacher ordered

they both then got back to how they were with Isaac stood only a few inches from Luna said his line again standing there a bit confused as to what to do

"RICHARDS PLEASE JUST KISS THE GIRL" the teacher ordered

He turned from Luna's face but didn't actually move

"can't I just-" he began

"oh for god sake Isaac" Luna said before grabbing his face with both her hands and kissing him for a full few 30 seconds he was in utter shock he didn't even kiss back but it did silence Mr dentrodelteatro for a moment till Luna pulled away leaving Isaac confused and happy he gave a small laugh then fell on the floor having obviously fainted "IS HE ALIGHT?" Mr dentrodelteatro said sounding quite concerned

"I think so he is fine when he gets up" Luna answered at that moment the bell rang indicating the return to rooms

"Anyone know where his room is?" Mr Dentrodelteatro asked

"I do" Luna said

"Harrison help Luna get Isaac back to his room" Mr Dentrodelteatro said

Harrison then turned from the door and walk back to the stage and stood with Luna "hey there Luna" he said with a smirk on his face

"Hey, can you give me a hand" she replied

"Sure" he answered they both took an arm of Isaac and got him up he was still passes out they walked him back to the room dropping him on his bed

"So, what me to walk you to your room Luna?" he asked
"Be a short walk you're in it" she laughed
"What you two are like together then?" he asked
"no-well sort of we are strangers meet a few weeks ago on
the first day we got here but we are roommates and
pretty good mates I guess" Luna said sitting on her bed
"So are you two not an item?" he asked
"No not even close I don't think" she answered
"What's that" he pointed to the bear next to Isaac's
sleeping head
"Oh that's Isaac's teddy bear he uh he can't sleep without
it" she said
"Aww that is adorable" he said
"I guess yeah" she sighed
"Well I guess I will see you on Friday Luna look after him
for me" he said
"Sure" she answered
he gave her a wink then left the room shutting the door
behind him Luna then got up from her bed and sat with
Isaac he was still out cold till she stared poking him till
he started to turn in his sleep and start she assumed he
was taking in his sleep "oh go away mum I want to
dream" he said
"No Isaac you have to wake up" she said mimicking his
mother's voice making her giggle a little
"Oh but mum I was having a lovely dream" he said
cuddling his pillow still with his eyes shut
"Oh what about Isaac?" she asked still using his mother's
voice
"about a girl and she kissed me" he was clearly still
dreaming   his eye's still closed and he drifted in and out
of sleep with each word he almost bundled himself with
that sentence looking really happy
"Oh what was she like?" she asked
"the most beautiful girl I ever saw, but she does see

much in me she thinks I a baby" he then went back to sleep, Luna left him alone for a minute to check he was still asleep till she slapped his face bringing him back to full awareness's and sitting up

"What- how did I get here I was acting a second ago" he asked
"You fainted Isaac me and Harrison brought you back here you idiot" she said
"Oh why...why did I faint" he asked
"Think back Isaac" she said
She could see the intense though he was going through till he obviously realised what happened and his mouth opened and almost dropped to the ground

"Oh my god we uh- we uh....we uh we-" he stuttered
"Yes we did Isaac" she said
He looked very blank for a second before he spoke again
"So uh is Mr Dentrodelteatro happy with our acting"
"Well he is a bit annoyed you fainted I think but not doing that will come with practice" she said
"PRACTICE, WE ARE DOING THAT AGAIN" he said very shocked and worried
"Yes Isaac we are gunna do it again on Friday" she said
he sat for a moment a bit worried then turned to face Luna now sitting on her bed "wait a second you kissed me not me kiss you like the script said" he said
"I know that" she replied
"Why did you do that?" he asked
"Many reasons" she said
"Like?" he asked
"like to get the scene done, to make you shut up about it, to get Mr dentrodelteatro of your back I don't know I just did okay take it any way you want" she said
"Anyway I want?" he asked more to himself
"Except that way" she said
"What way?" he asked

"You know perfectly well what way not to take it" she sighed

"I have to go see Jake a minuet" he said in a panic

Isaac then left and practically ran into Jakes room he was sat putting some food into the spider tank and looking up at him in surprise "hey Isaac what do you want today" Jake asked

"Something either horrible or brilliant happened today" Isaac answered

"Okay what happened Isaac" Jake asked

"Well we were going thought a scene in our performance and..." Isaac trailed off

"And Isaac what " Jake asked trying to make Isaac get to the point

"And Luna kissed me" Isaac said bluntly

"Really oh my god man what did you do" Jake asked

"I....uh...." Isaac trailed off again

"What did you do Isaac" Jake asked

"I fainted" Isaac said a bit ashamed

"You fainted" Jake asked

"Yes" Isaac answered

"You're both in it and screwed man" Jake said

"How so" Isaac asked calming down a bit now

"Well in this production of yours you get to kiss her I guess a lot and so you're in but if you fainted and that mattered and changed in anyway her opinion of you your doomed" Jake answered

"Yes I got that much Jake" Isaac said

"So what did you come to see me for then" Jake asked

"What the hell do I do now" Isaac asked

"just chill Isaac try discussing it and see where that lead's you but you got to stop asking me for help with this stuff really I know more about your feeling for her then you do" Jake suggested

"good point, thank you" Isaac said before running of back to the room seeing Luna now stood making dinner in the small kitchen area and setting it on the table "hello" he said as he got back

"Oh good your back come on it's time for dinner" she answered

He sat on the table the food was simple it was a quick dinner for a late night they sat and ate in silence till Isaac broke the silence

"So about today" he asked

"What about it Isaac" she asked

"About what happened today" he asked

"Go on" she sighed

"Look I don't want to imply anything but uh- that was a lot of heat for an acting kiss Luna" he suggested rather slyly

"Really how would you know" she asked

"Good point but still I guess I'm sorry" he said

"Sorry for what" she asked

"What happened if I wasn't being stupid and had just got it over with I probably wouldn't have fainted and have to put you thought the embarrassment and stuff" he said

"Relax Isaac you're the one that will have to deal with embarrassment know not me" she laughed

"True, I'm never gunna live this down am I" he asked

"No but I would be more concerned that Harrison known's you sleep with a teddy bear" she laughed

"Oh god I'm doomed I will be a laughing stock" he said

"It's okay it could be worse" she reassured him

"how, the whole theatre sore me kiss a girl then faint, then Harrison found out I sleep with a bear I don't see how it could be worse" he said

"You could also find out that a certain someone known's what you said in your sleep before you woke up from your faint" she giggled

"Wait what" he asked very worried

"About the beautiful girl that see's nothing in you" she said

"Please don't tell me I said that out loud" he asked

panicking

"Yep you did" she giggled

"Oh my god I'm so dead" he said putting his head in his hands

"Relax Isaac I won't say a word about whomever it was you meant" she laughed

"Luna" he said

"Yes Isaac" she replied

"Can we practice that scene again?" he asked

"No we can't, I'm tired and want to go to sleep" she answered

"Fine but can I ask you something" he asked

"Sure shoot Isaac" she replied

"On a scale of one to ten, how was that in your opinion" he asked

Luna just looked at him for a moment she looked up into his eye's looking at them though his glasses before getting up from her seat and moving across the room and sitting on her bed he then went and sat with her

"You didn't answer my question Luna scale of one to ten tell me" he said

"Fine about a high four or low five" she answered

"What" he asked

"You heard me" she replied

"I thought I did better than that" he sighed sounding rather down about that

"Relax not like it really matter's" she said

"What if it does matter?" he asked

"Do you want a re call?" she asked

"A what-" he asked confused

before he could finish just like in the theatre she pressed her lip's against his this time he began almost instantly kissing back his hand's snaked around her waist her hands moved to his neck they both tilted their head's slightly deepening the kiss till Luna pulled away much to the annoyance of Isaac who seemed to have been really enjoying himself for a while

"Okay time for bed I think before you get to existed" she said

"What out of ten was that" he asked

"Seven" she answered

"Seven?" he asked a bit annoyed it was so low still

"Yep, there is always room for improvement Isaac" she laughed

Isaac then jumped over on to his bed and sat there till Luna had changed in the bathroom and got into bed Isaac then followed suit and sat up in his bed for a while

"hey Luna are you still up" he whispered

"Of course I am Isaac what do you want" she said

"I was just thinking.... because ...you know your bed look's.... really big and stuff.... if I could uh-" he said

"No Isaac goes to sleep" she shouted at him

"Okay...but maybe if I-" he asked

"No" she said

A few seconds later the almost exact thing happened again and again for another four times till

"Luna" he said

"No Isaac goes to sleep or I will knock you out with a frying pan" she complained

"Oh come on please one night I swear" he asked

"No" she said

"Please" he begged

"No Isaac" she said

"Pretty please" he begged

"Will you go to sleep if I say yes" she asked

"Yes" he answered

"Fine, but on one condition" she said

"What condition" he asked

"The bear stay's there" she said

"Oh come on Luna" he complained

"No one or the other Isaac not both, you either sleep with the bear or you sleep with me not both" she said

"Fine," he then held up the bear so he could look it in its eyes "my lord I it gives me great sorrow that I must now leave your arms to go to the arms of another-"
"No you're not" Luna interrupted
"okay to the bed of another, goodbye my friend" he then gave the bear a kiss and put the bear in his bed all tucked in and everything before claiming into the side of Luna's bed he instantly tried to wrap his arm around her but she just pushed him away and sat up slightly "Isaac for mental note my side of the bed" she said indicating to the half of the bed she was laying on

"Your side of the bed" she said indicating to the side he was laying

"And at no point will you or any part of you cross over to this side and nothing of mine will pass you that side" she said

"I don't know I wouldn't mind if certain bits of you were on my side of the bed" he said slyly walking his fingers up her side

"Isaac shut it" she said gripping his hand and crushing it making him squeal before turning away he waited a few minutes before wrapping his arms around her going right up close to her so his head was on her shoulder and his front was up close to her back so there wasn't an inch between them but she just pushed him of the bed completely and onto the floor "ow" he said as he hit the floor

"Serves you right" she said

He then just got back into Luna's bed again staying on his side for a while before wrapping his arms around her again

"ISAAC" she said turning to face him

"What?" he asked

"My side, your side, if I catch you on my side of the bed again I will cut of whatever is on my side" she said he moved to be completely on his side almost falling of the end of the bed

"Thank you" she said turning away again

"Can I have a goodnight kiss Luna?" he asked innocently she then turned and gave him a kiss yet he turned it into snogging with her arms around his neck and his around her waist while they were kissing he tried to move his hands up slightly to feel the bottom of her bra
"DON'T YOU DARE!" she said making him pull his hands away from her as they kissed.

Chapter 6

First to wake was Luna slowly rising out of bed to notices Isaac's arm was round her again she slowly rolled over so she was facing him and started tapping him and repeating his name till he woke up he got his glasses and looked at his phone and noticed that the alarm had been going off for about two and half hours they were too late to the class to go now so they both decried to have a lazy day they didn't even get dressed they just sat up in Luna's bed watching day time TV
"You know something Luna" he asked
"What do I or do I not know Isaac" she sighed
"Daytime TV is awful" he said
"Yes it is well what else are we gunna do all day it's not even lunch yet" she asked

"I don't know, maybe does more theatre work" he
suggested
"No I made a vow when I woke up this morning I was
having a lazy day I'm not doing any work" she said
"Fine then what do you want to do?" he said
"I don't know, what do you?" she asked
"I want to discuss the sleeping arrangements" he said
"What do you mean?" she asked worried about the
answer
"Well in short that was the best night sleep I have ever
had and now I have slept in the wonder of this bed I
don't what to go back to that one" he said
"NO Isaac you said one night" she replied very angry now
"Oh come on Luna I'm not hurting anybody am I" he
complained
"it's not that Isaac, what if someonc was to come in
looking for us or something how would we explain 'oh yes
we were sleeping in the same bed after what most people
know what happened yesterday but there is nothing
going on' to people Isaac" she said
"But people expect us to be doing much more than we
are" he replied
"I know but you said one night, one night is over own bed
tonight Isaac" she told him
"Fine, I need a cig you coming" he asked
"Sure" she sighed
they both went onto the balcony and shared a cigarette
they didn't say much, after that the day went pretty fast
doing nothing at all they both new they had to get up and
work tomorrow they only had three more Wednesdays of
work before the English and maths courses where
finished and Wednesdays becomes a work day for
homework or for extra classes or activity's Isaac did put
up another fight about sleeping in his own bed again
having no effect, unfortunately it was quiet a cold night
there was under floor heating in their room but it wasn't
very good both of them sat in there bed's freezing till

Luna spoke "Isaac are you still awake"
"Of course I am it's freezing in here" he said the sound of him shivering obvious from his voice
"Well there is not much we can do about it till they fix the heating" she sighed in reply
"I swear it better be fixed by December" he said
Isaac then got his phone it was difficult for him to tell the time till he put his glasses on he could now Luna laying on the other side of his bed looking at him obviously just claimed into bed with him "I thought you said I couldn't sleep with you tonight" he asked
"I said you couldn't sleep in my bed I said nothing about yours now shut up its cold" she said
Isaac took her hand she was colder than he was they crossed each of their blankets
"Have you decided yet" Luna asked
"Decided what" he asked
"If you're staying over Christmas and stuff Isaac" she asked
"Of course I have, im staying here with you, no way im going home, I will never come back" he laughed
Luna gave him a hit playfully and they both laughed then either as a sudden boost of confidence or just being stupid Isaac put his arm around Luna pulling her closer so now almost inches a part in resonance she put her head into his neck and rested her cold hands on his chest he then took of his glasses and they both laid there happy together
"Im happy I found you Luna" he said
"Im happy I found you Isaac" she replied "goodnight Isaac"
"Goodnight Luna" they both then kissed and went to sleep in each other's arms. after that day life for Luna and Isaac became very much the same thing just lesson's and learning and acting then going back to the room for TV or gaming, a cuddle and a brilliant night sleep till a few week's latter when it was Friday they just got back

from theatre after doing a rather active scene for them both when they just walked into the room and collapsed onto Isaac's bed with a sigh "that was difficult" he said
"Yep and for once not because of us" she replied
"Yeah it was Harrison and Mel messing up not us" he sighed
"I know I have never done one scene so many times in my life" she laughed
"I know I don't think I have kisses you that much in such a short period of time" he said
"You didn't seem to mind" she laughed
"True, but come on it was getting ridiculous how many times did we do there entrance" he asked
"32 times Isaac" she answered
"Wow, that seems low" he said
"We did there entrance 32 times but the whole sccnc 43 times" she sighed
"That sounds more like it" he sighed
"Don't complain so much" she said playfully hitting him
"Im not relax but that was it no more stuff now till after Christmas" he said
"YAY luckily we are not going anywhere" she said
"True" he replied
"By the way what was up with Mel today" she asked
"Oh, I don't think she has quiet grasped what's really going on, and she keep's trying to flirt with me" he said
"Really, you're in there Isaac" she laughed
"Shut up Luna you know me, I wouldn't do that would I" he said wrapping his arms around her
"no you wouldn't" she replied before giving him a kiss and walking out for a cigarette Isaac then followed her out and they did as they did everyday shared a cigarette till Isaac got a phone call from his mother
"Hey mum-
Look what do you want-
You're kidding me
Please don't I beg you don't-

I can't believe you mum" he said as his half of the phone call
"What was all that about?" Luna asked
"You know I told you about Melissa Harding" he said sounding both worried and guilty
"Yeah what about her" Luna asked
"my mother has sent her on a plane here she is on her way now just landed apparently with my mother as well" he sighed
"Crap what are we gunna do now" she asked
"Like we always do nothing" he said
"How's that gunna work" she asked
"I don't know, but it's the best plan we've got" he said
"How long we got" she asked
"About half an hour" he answered
"Great are they intending to say here or what" she asked
"I think she intends to try and guilt trip me into going home and staying there" he said
"Well do you have any feeling's for her does she have any for you" she asked
"I hate her, she has a huge crush on me" he answered
"Well this is gunna go down well isn't it" she sighed
"Yes I rather think it will, it will be a surprise for my mother that's for sure" he said laughing slightly
"Well if you don't like her why would guilt tripping you work" she asked
"It won't, im staying here with you even if she find's my dad and order's me home im staying here with you an no one can change that" he said
"Isaac stops acting like that" she said turning away from him slightly
"Like what?" he asked
"All lovey dovey you know I don't do lovey dovey" she said sounding sick of the idea
"I know you don't Luna that's not the point no matter what she does to me your my girl not her" he said wrapping his arms around her again

"Okay" she sighed wrapping her arms around his neck a bit lazily

They then kissed on the balcony till they heard a familiar voice on the balcony next to them it was Jake "I so called it" he said

"What did you call Jake?" Luna asked

"I said first day I meet the two of you first day you meet I said and I quote   'if something does catch on I will be the one to say I called it first' and look what I spot" Jake said

"Oh shut up Jake mind your own business" Isaac said keeping Luna close to him

"Luna helps me out here" Jake pleaded

"No Jake mind your own business Isaac inside now" she said pointing to inside Isaac then did as he was told

Jake then got his phone and used a whip sound app making Luna giggle

"Shut up Jake" he shouted back from inside obviously having seen it

when they went back into the room they cleaned up a bit not a lot needed cleaning but it   just made it slightly better as they didn't know how long his mother intended on being there till they heard the sound of a high pitched British accent and familiar sound of his mother when hearing the impending doom the just sat cuddled together watching the TV when the door opened it was them his mother looked the same as before dressed all in black with her nose in the air her eyes fixed on Isaac and a rather small thin girl with bleach blonde hair about a pound of make up on and the shortest skirt on earth and a pair of high heels her eye's when to Isaac then looked to Luna and her face welled up with anger just looking at her "can I help you" Isaac said glaring at his mother

"yes you can you can help us and help yourself Isaac for the last time im asking this pack your things and come home with me and your future wife" his mother ordered

"No, mum im not going anywhere I told you before I am staying here with Luna Redgrave" he said

"Then please Luna Redgrave take your hands of my husband you little whore" Melissa said
"What did you call me?" Luna said incredibly calmly but Isaac of course by now knew better and removed his arm from around knowing full well what was going to happen
"I called you a whore" she replied
Luna just walked up to her calmly and put her hand to her neck placing her about half way up the way with no escape
"I would be very careful what you say to me Melissa" Luna said increasing her grip slightly everyone in the room even Isaac was shocked "now I would suggest taking it back"
"I-I-I-I-im sorry" she choked
"Sorry what?" Luna said though her teeth
"Sorry Miss Redgrave" she said
Luna then just let go and let her fall to the ground as Luna sat back down with Isaac putting her head into his neck he then put his arm around her and didn't even give his mother a glance "miss Redgrave would you mind leaving while I talk to my son" his mother said
"Anything you have to say to me you can say to her" Isaac said not removing his stare from the TV
"No Isaac I must insist she leaves so I can't talk to you" his mother ordered
"Fine" Luna said getting up and walking to the balcony, Jake was still stood on his balcony but with a new cigarette
"What the hell is going on in there?" he asked
"Isaac's mother had turned up again with his..." she trailed off
"His what?" he asked
"There engaged or something like that she's his future wife" she said
"Wow he didn't tell you" he said
"No I knew he just told me he hand no feeling's for her and that he hated her" she replied

"So what are you doing out here" he asked

"His mother wants to talk to him alone for a minuet" she sighed

"Wow tough break Luna" he said

"I know you don't have to remind me Jake" she replied

"Sorry Luna but remember you did say you couldn't let him get into something he can't get you of easily" he said

"I know it's just hard that's all" she sighed

"How is it hard Luna im sure if Isaac does really feel that way about you he won't care what danger he's in" he added

"I know it's just I might have to do something soon and it will smash him to pieces" she sighed

"Luna, you don't get it do you, I mean you could say all this started from that kiss but I know a little different, almost every night Isaac would come see me to talk about you and he would phase the floor in my room thinking what he was gunna do that day to make it different and special, I mean he told me once that he's happy he didn't run of sooner and go on that tour like he original planed they he wouldn't have meet you the way he did and he once said that if he had done like he did originality and did the moonlight course it would have been the worse decision he ever made" he said

"Really" she asked

"yep he told me that once he's crazy, much crazier then you could ever be Luna no matter what the problem is I know you two can fix it together" he said

"Maybe your right, but what if your wrong what it like I think the problem can't be fixed" she sighed

"Then you can try your best to mend it" he said

"Thanks' Jake" she said

Chapter 7

Luna then went back in the room to see Isaac laid side

way's on the bed crying his face was bleeding it was obvious by the way his mother was standing by the bed that she had hit him "get the hell out" Luna said though her teeth

"How dare you order me around Miss Redgrave" his mother said rather shocked that someone would talk to her like that

"yeah if I was you Mrs Richards I would have Googled that name now GET OUT OF MY HOUSE before I really lose my temper with you and that slut friend of yours now get out" Luna said

she then left in a huff acting like the queen before slamming the door shut Luna then locked it and ran back to Isaac he sat now holding his head he had a small cut on the top of his head "oh my god Isaac, im so sorry" she said

"No don't be it's not your fault Luna is mine" he replied

"What did she do?" she asked

"She hit me with her bag" he answered

"Why?" she asked

"I told her to leave me alone to let me live my own life and to let me be with you and she hit me not the first time she's done that" he sighed

"Well she's not here dear but try the class rooms or something if shc come's I will tell her you're looking for her"

Luna then got some medial stuff from the bathroom to check Isaac would be okay

"What the hell do you mean not the first time she's done that" Luna asked while just cleaning the small cut on his head

"Back at home if I ever used to think for myself then I would get left with something to remember my mistake with" he sighed

"That's horrible Isaac" she said

"Well im used to it" he sighed

"no you don't have to be used to that Isaac no way" Luna

said hugging him Isaac took a second before griping her tightly like he never wanted to let go till Luna pulled away just enough to see his face he still looked like he was crying a bit "I-uh really need to talk to you about something" Luna said rather sharply

"Sure anything, what is it" he asked

"Question one- yes or no do you like me" she asked

"Of course I do" he said like she had just asked him if one plus one was two

"Okay, but do you love me" she asked

"How the hell could I not Luna" he answered

With every sentence Luna said she looked more worried and now kept glancing at the door

"But you know Isaac that you don't know stuff about me" she said sounding very distracted

"I know all I need to know don't I" he asked

Luna said nothing for a moment

"Don't I Luna?" he asked

"Of course you do Isaac all you need to know but even if something happened like me having to disappear" she said

"Then we would disappear together" he answered

"What if we can't?" she said

"Luna what's the matter with you, come on something is wrong and I think I need to know what it is" he said

"No you don't Isaac you don't want to know what it is okay can we please just leave it at that" she said sounding very uptight and upset by this topic

"No Luna we can't just leave it at that I think I need to know what the woman I love is talking about" he said

"please Isaac don't" Luna then started to cry Isaac pulled her to his chest so she was crying into him and tried to calm her down when she did he pulled her away enough to look straight into her green eye's "Luna I don't care what you may or may not have done all right if you don't what to tell me you don't have to" he said

"Thank you Isaac" she replied

"It's okay, I love you enough to not put you though it if it meant that much to you" he said

"I love you Isaac" she replied

"I know now come on let's get some sleep" he said

"Okay" she sighed

the next day Isaac woke up first as usual to find Luna was nowhere in the room he checked everywhere he began to panic he ran out and burst in Jake's door he was sat with his spider but that didn't deter Isaac from classical screaming at him "LUNA'S GONE"

Jake then put the spider back in its tank before running into Isaac and Luna's room he looked around and checked the bathroom everything was empty

"Where was she last you sore her Isaac" Jake said calmly

"Uh last night she was in bed with me I woke up this morning and she's gone" he replied franticly

"Right when did you fall asleep" Jake asked

"Around 11 I think" Isaac answered

"Right and it's now 8 am so we know she can't be far away the gate's only opened an hour ago" Jake said still sounding very calm

"Well then where is she" Isaac said sounding very worried

"I don't know check your phone" Jake suggested

Isaac ran over and checked his phone no messages and no missed call's

"Nothing" Isaac said holding his phone screen so Jake could see it

"Uh try to call her" Jake said

Isaac then set up his phone to call her as it rang he could here another sound they both looked around till Jake found Luna's phone under the pillow Isaac then stopped ringing it

"It's all fault" Isaac said

"What, how can it be your fault Isaac" Jake asked

"I, I, I tried to make her tell me about stuff and she said what if she had to disappear" Isaac explained

"What you think that's what's happened you think she's

ran of" Jake asked

"Well what else could it be" Isaac asked

"Isaac you know Luna what other than her phone is still here" Jake asked

he looked around the room at all the places Luna usually put's her stuff and everything was still there he money all her clothes everything was still there Isaac then began to panic even more

"Where could she be" Jake said more to himself

"Julia" Isaac said out of the blue

"What?" Jake asked

"Luna's aunt lives on campus she's the only alliterative but Luna wouldn't have gone to see her willingly and even if she had to go see her she would have dragged me with her" Isaac explained

"What if it was personal she needed to speak to hcr aunt about" Jake said

"What do you mean" Isaac asked

Jake then gave him a look that sort of overly suggestive look

"You said that her aunt was there for everything from bullies to....pregnancy" Jake said

"No Jake it wouldn't have been that" Isaac answered

"Why not?" Jake asked

"Has not happened yet" Isaac said

"Wow, what's your hold up" Jake asked

"Right now the fact she's missing I think is a good answer" Isaac answered

"Okay but I think your best bet
 Is either go see her aunt or stay here and wait" Jake said

"hang on we need to check something give me a sec" Isaac said as he ran into the bathroom but some dirty clothes on quickly then told Jake to follow him and ran out the door and straight out the building "where are we going" Jake asked

"To check something" Isaac answered

they both then walked to the student car park "right my bike is still here okay that's one idea gone" they then walked to the lecturers car park to see her aunt's car still there "okay one more idea gone" they then walked off to Julia's room they knocked on the door getting no answer he then knocked again when Julia then opened the door hardly dressed she didn't kiss him she just looked at him confused "have you seen Luna" he said franticly

"No why darling" she replied sounding very tired

"I can't find her" he said

"What, why what's happened dear" she asked

"I sort of upset her last night and I woke up this morning she was gone left all her stuff now we can't find her" he said

"Well she's not here dear try the class rooms if she comes here I will tell her your looking for her" she answered

"Thanks" he said

She then shut the door "well what now" Jake said

"You go back to the room in case she comes back I will go to our classes see if she's there" Isaac answered

"okay man good luck" Jake said then walked of back to the room's and Isaac ran off to the English and maths rooms but no sign of her then to the media with the same result he then began panicky running around campus looking at everyone and everything till he got to the theatre as he stepped in he could she someone in a black shirt and jeans passing on the stage as he ran down the aisle to the stage and jumped on it he could see it   was Luna he ran up and hugged her almost crying onto her shoulder just repeating meaning less sentences "morning Isaac are you all right" she asked

"Yes im fine why are you not" he said franticly

"Im fine you're not though relax calm down what's the matter" she asked

"I thought you had dispersed" he said

"No why would I have dispersed" she said

"After what you said last night and then I wake up to find

your gone without a trace what did you expect me to think" he said

"Oh im sorry Isaac, I should have told you where I was going" she replied

"It's okay at least I found you now, what are you doing here" he asked

"Oh just practising some dialogue that's all" she answered

Isaac then looked at the page her script was on "but we rehearsed this up stair's didn't we" he said

"I know but our room doesn't quite match the theatre for echo and sound and stuff" she said

"Oh okay I guess but please don't do that again okay" he said

"Okay I know" she stood up and gave him a small kiss calming him down more

"Do you need me for your rehearsing" he asked

"Not at the moment Isaac" she answered

"Okay" he then jumped of the stage and sat in the front row looking all existed

"What are you doing Isaac" she asked looking at him over the top of her glasses

"Im being and audience" he answered

"You can't be an audience on your own" she told him

"Then im an audient" he said

"Fine" she said continuing to re-site a final monologue for Isabella that went something like this:

"Not once not twice I have witnessed this but a million times

Why bother a courting for love when my only chance at it flies away

What point is it to wait around day after day for a lovely gentlemen when

Others wait not but ten seconds for one, or am I just not worth it to them

all my time I have lied in wait for the man I love to take the chance and when he does it all messes up, why bother all men now won't touch me im to old now for courting and im still to young enough to join witchcraft I have nowhere to go, I have made myself impossible waiting for the man I love just to be still alone by the end of it, I feel not but used was he really different or is my mind just playing tricks to fake not but forgiveness to him."

"That was brilliant Luna" Isaac said as soon as she finished

"Thank you Isaac, come on your go your monologue is next come on" Luna said as she left the stage and Isaac when on with this script:

"how could I have done that, my one chance frown away because of one stupid mistake a mistake that wasn't even me, I wish apron the god's for forgiveness but it is no use I have not wasted the only person I care for on this green earth, and in have lost her forever now, why, why, why the hell did I listen to my stupid brother if I had not none of this would have happened I may as well end it all now I have naught to live for without her"

"That was lovely Isaac" Luna said as soon as he finished

"Thank you Luna" he answered "what should we do now" he asked

"I don't know maybe play a game" she said

"Like?" he asked

"Like....truth or dare" she answered

"Really" he asked

"yep truth or dare im sold" she said as she claimed back onto the stage and they both sat down crossed legged facing each other "okay I will go first truth or dare Isaac" Luna said

"I think truth" he said

"Okay... how long had you liked me before I kissed you?" she asked

"Uh quite a while" he said a bit guilty

"Need a date or close enough Isaac" she said

"Fine about a three days after I met you" he replied

Luna just laughed at him for a minuet

"Truth or dare Luna" he asked

"Truth" she said

"Okay...how long had you liked me before you kissed me" he asked

"About a well I think it probably when you had to take your shirt of in class, truth or dare Isaac" she asked

"I think dare" he said

"Okay... oh I dare you to call Jake and tell him you love him" she giggled

"What no way am I doing that" he said

"If you don't you have to do the for fit" she said

"Which is" he asked

"To spend a week with my aunt and Jake's spider in a small room" she threatened

"Oh god I don't know what's worse" he said

"Tell Jake you love him or spend time with my aunt and a spider your choice Isaac" she giggled

"Fine" he said getting his phone from his pocket and dialling Jake then putting it on a speaker phone "hey Jake" he said

"Hey Isaac, find Luna" Jake asked

"Yep I found her in the theatre" Isaac said

"Well good we found her then" Jake said

"Yep but there was a second part to this call something I have to tell you" Isaac said

"Okay Isaac what, what's happened" Jake said worried

"No nothing's happened I just...uh....I love you Jake" Isaac said quietly

Luna then just burst into a fit of laughter Isaac just looking angrier by the second

"Im sorry Isaac what did you say?" Jake asked

Luna just smirked at him he could see in her face she was hinting at the spider and her aunt if he didn't finish the phone call

"I was just saying im in love with you" Isaac said

"Sorry Isaac where you talking to Luna or me" Jake

asked

"Im talking to you Jake" Isaac said

"Im sorry did I miss something important here I think I did" Jake asked

Luna just burst out laughing "sorry Jake, Luna and me are playing truth or dare I was dared to call you and say that I loved you im so sorry Jake"

"It is fine get back to your game" he then hung up

He then practically jumped on Luna pinning her to the floor "you little...there is no word to describe you Luna" he said

"Sorry I but it was pretty funny" she laughed

"No it wasn't funny im never doing that again" he said sternly

"So many things on your never gunna do again list isn't there they Isaac" she laughed

"Yes because there is lots people make me do that I don't always want to do" he answered

"Yeah like taking your top of and talking to certain people and saying things" she laughed

"For once shut up Luna" he said to her

"No Isaac I will not shut up" she said

"Though truth or dare Luna" he asked

"Truth" she answered

"Okay would you rather spend a million years with a spider or the rest of your life with your aunt and no one else" he asked

"Option one" she answered

"Really you would rather live a million years with a spider then the rest of your life alone with your aunt" he asked

"Yes" she answered

"Why?" he asked

"Because... options one I can still see you" she said

"Aww, but oh no you won't if you have a spider you're not coming anywhere near me" he replied

"Thanks Isaac your gunna abandon me because I may have a spider with me" she laughed

"Maybe" he said more as a joke

She hit him playfully till they both sat up again after a while they both got bored and decided to go back to the room when they got there Jake was sat on Luna's bed

"what are you still doing here?" Isaac said

"I wanted to tell you guy's something" Jake said

"What Jake?" Luna asked

"Im leaving I won't be back till after the new year" Jake said

"Okay well I guess see you after the holiday's Jake" Luna said

"Yep but Isaac private chat next door" Jake said

"okay" Isaac replied he gave Luna a kiss before they both went next door Jake told Isaac to sit down on the bed next to a couple of suit cases for him uncomfortably close to the spider it seemed to move in its tank to it could be only a few inches from Isaac and it keep moving, his eye's fixed on it till Jake started talking quite quietly

"So Isaac I want to talk to you about something" Jake said

"Sure what" Isaac asked

"You and Luna" Jake said

"Can you be more specific" Isaac asked

"Okay what has happened, what you want to happen and what other subjects must I cover before I go" Jake said

"Okay what has happened, not a lot just the fact we kiss and share the same bed is it really" Isaac said

"Okay right what do you want to happen and is it possible" Jake asked

"What do you mean by that Jake" Isaac asked

"Fine sub-question. Are you a virgin?" Jake asked

"Yes" Isaac answered

"Is she?" Jake asked

"Yes" Isaac answered

"Do you not want to be?" Jake asked

"Yes" Isaac answered

"Are you gunna answer yes to everything?" Jake asked

"No" Isaac answered
"Okay do you know or have any idea how to do that?"
Jake asked
"No" Isaac answered
"right that gives us a starting point then...so what
happens is that when a man loves a woman there will be
moments when he gets certain   feelings in his-" Jake
began
"Jake I know that bit my mother did tell me that bit, I
mean my mum wanted me to have six kids of course I
know how to do it but I just never actually tried and I
don't know the social logic to doing it"   Isaac interrupted
"right... then I guess if you have a problem work it out
because im not gunna be here to help you and it is
proverbial I will come back with a girlfriend so no more
bursting in at all hours to rant at me okay" Jake said
"Okay can I just ask one thing though" Isaac asked
"Sure shoot Isaac" Jake said
"The one bit my mother never explained I assumed it was
like a dad thing to explain but uh if I get a...." he tailed of
thinking of a way to really say it without saying it
"A what Isaac" Jake asked
"You know what I mean...uh" Isaac just indicated to Jake
what he meant by looking at his own pants
"oh you mean a-"" Jake said understanding
"Yes that, what do I do?" Isaac asked
"Uh good question Isaac" Jake said unsure of how to
really answer it
"well, what do I do if me and Luna are doing something
and that happens I am of course extreamly familiar with
doing it myself but what do I do to well let her know or
whatever what do I do about it" Isaac asked
"   well I mean if you notice and so does she and your
both all good with it it's not really your thing to deal with
its more her to worry about" Jake answered
"Really" Isaac asked
"Yes I think so but if she doesn't go to your bathroom,

bathrooms will soon become your best friend, I can't believe this wasn't explained in school to you Isaac by at least other boys and their girlfriends" Jake said

"no I went to an all boy boarding school no girls allowed within three miles of the premises unless direct family even then they needed permission"   Isaac answered

"Wow, no wonder you're so ill educated" Jake joked

"Are we done?" Isaac asked

"Yes I think so no more problems though okay" Jake said

"Okay cheers Jake have a nice break" Isaac said

"See you two when I get back" Jake said

Isaac then left and returned to the room to see Luna sat on the bed with her laptop just playing a game he assumed till she notice him and dropped the screen down in a flash and put it away "what's up Luna" he asked

"Nothing...nothing Isaac why what was all that about" she asked

"Nothing important guy stuff" he said sitting next to her she looked distracted like there was something on her mind

"You sure you're okay" he asked

"Of course I am why wouldn't I be" she said

"I don't know you just looked it that's all" he said

"Im fine Isaac stop asking about it" she said shoving him slightly she then looked at him strangely before speaking "your shirts on inside out Isaac" she said

"Well I was sort of in a rush this morning considering I thought you'd dispersed of the face of the earth" he said

"Well I hadn't I was still around wasn't I " she said

"I know I just panicked is all" he replied

"Can you please fix your shirt it's bugging the hell out of me" she asked

"Sure" he sighed

He then took of his shirts before noticing there was nothing wrong with them

"My shirts are fine Luna" he said

"I know I just kinda wanted to see you with your shirt of again" she smirked

Isaac just laughed at her "your evil sometimes with evil intentions" he said

"I know" she giggled

"am im half UN dressed I may as well shower" Isaac said getting up and going into the bathroom when he had left Luna got her laptop again she opened up her emails to see a new email from not a name but a number and her face turned white she looked around the room and getting up still with her laptop in her hands she walked to the bathroom door and could hear Isaac singing in the shower so she sat back down and opened the email it simply had lots of letters and numbers on it she gazed at them all for a considerable amount of time so long in fact Isaac had now gotten out the shower got changed and walked back into the room sitting on the bed beside her looking over her shoulder before she even notice he was there "what's that" he asked

"Just something okay" she said

"Well what Luna is it important" he asked

"Sort of" she replied

"But it's just a bunch of random letters and numbers right" he asked

"Yep" she said

"So how is it important" he asked

"It's not" she said

"But didn't you just say-" he began

"Can we not do this please not tonight okay" she asked

"Well is it something I should worry about or not" he asked

"No it isn't" she said

"Okay just asking is all, so what's tonight's plan then" he asked

"Uh... nothing" she said still not moving her gave from the screen

"Really didn't we do anything yesterday" he joked

"I know but I want to do nothing again I like nothing" she said still not moving her gaze from the screen
"Sure fine" he sighed
and they did nothing for quite a few day's each day Luna would have her head glued to the laptop screen at that same email from the second Isaac was awake to the second he went to sleep he hadn't seen her not looking at it for at least four day's till eventually Isaac spoke up
"look Luna I know it's not important and that im sure I don't want to know but what is that thing you pay more attention to it then you do to me" he said
"No I don't" Luna answered still not removing her eyes from the screen
"Luna will you at least look at me" he asked now getting angry at her
Luna moved her eye's for a second to look at him then returned them to the screen again "Luna im serious, what's more important to you, a random email that doesn't even make scene or the man how loves you" he asked
Luna didn't answer her eyes still glued to the screen not even giving him a glance "LUNA" he shouted
"What Isaac?" she replied still not looking at him
"Can you please answer me?" he asked
she darted her eyes at him then back the screen again her face still lacking of any emotional sign till Isaac gave up he got up shut the laptop lid down and moved it to the other bed Luna still hadn't moved or changed her gaze from where the screen was till Isaac knelled on the floor so his face was where the screen was "Luna please I haven't seen your eyes of that screen for a week what is that" he asked
"It's nothing Isaac nothing" she said
"Don't lie to me Luna what is it or more importantly who is it" he asked
"It's....it's" she stuttered not wanting to tell him
"Who is it Luna" he asked

"It's Danny" she said

Chapter 7

"What the hell are you talking about" he asked
"It's Danny that's all nothing to worry about" she said
"Well I am worried about you Luna I thought you said
you didn't talk to him" he asked
"We don't, but he obviously sent this by accident I was
just checking it that's all" she said
"That's all?" he asked
"Yes" she answered
"Okay then but no more checking time to sleep Luna" he
told her
"Okay Isaac fine" she sighed
"thank you" he said as he gave her a kiss but seemed it
didn't seem to change or even move her face she just laid
back and fell asleep Isaac just sat on the other bed
looking at her for a while till he was sure she was asleep
he then got her laptop and opened it up it was luckily
still on the email it didn't look like anything to him but a
bunch of random letters and numbers all typed together
in no sore of sequence till right at the bottom it simply
said:" Danny has found you the boys arc coming code
1'200"
it all just seemed strange to him for a while till he
realised what that code most likely meant that Luna was
gunna have to disappear because someone was after her
he then put the laptop back to its original position and
ran out onto the balcony and stood gripping the pole
relentlessly looking out into the twilight just focusing on
not over panicking and making it obvious that he knew
about it maybe it was nothing or maybe it wasn't no
matter what way he put the situation it wasn't gunna be
a nice happy ending till it was early morning and he got
an idea that would either help fix the problem or make it

a lot worse he wasn't going to tell her if it really meant so much for him not to know it was bad that he knew as the day went on Luna still wasn't awake she looked dead to the world but she hadn't slept for a week so he didn't really mind after all Isaac didn't know how much time he had left before she had to disappear and no matter what they were doing he was gunna saver every second of it. He just simply claimed into bed beside her and held her tight till after a long time she woke up "hey Isaac"

Chapter 8

"Hey Luna, so what do you want to do today?" Isaac asked
"Nothing" she answered
"No, we have done nothing for weeks I want to do something" he complained
"Fine what do you want to do today Isaac?" she asked
"I want to go swimming" he suggested out of the blue
"How are we gunna do that" she asked
"Well campus has a pool and an indoor heated one two we could go swim in there" he suggested
"Really is that what you want to do today" she asked with a sigh
Isaac just nodded excitedly "okay" Luna replied after a long thought
"YES, but slight fault in my plan" he admitted
"And what's that Isaac" she asked crossing her arms
"I don't know how we are gunna get in or turn the stuff on etcetera" he explained
"Well how did you think I got in to the theatre, follow me" she said
Because they had both slept in their clothes they just got there swimming stuff and left. Luna then walked down a long path out to the UN explored side of campus till she stopped at a small door with lots of warnings and the

words go away written in red on it she knocked on the door and a tall lanky man with what may have been at one point blonde hair now just covered in dirt he looked Isaac up and down then looked to Luna "do you have the key to return" he asked in a low slow voice
"Yes but I have also have one to collect" she answered
"What one today, Miss Redgrave?" he asked
"Pool please" she answered
"Why do you want the pool key?" he asked
"Bored" she answered
The man looked at Isaac again then turned back to Luna "is he going with you?" he asked
"Yes he is" she answered
"Why?" he asked
"Because we are both bored" she answered
"Fine but I will be watching you Miss Redgrave and you Mr Richards"
He then took the theatre key from Luna then gave her another key "I want it back before 11PM please" he said
"Okay fine" she said
He then slammed the door in their faces
"Let's go" Luna said walking off and Isaac followed her
"What did he mean he would be watching us" Isaac asked
"Oh he's basically the groundskeepers, he keeps all the keys and watches all the cameras" she answered
"All the camera's, really" he asked
"Yep supposedly" she said
"Must be a happy man then" he joked
"I think so yes" she laughed
they both laughed till they found the indoor pool entrance it opened to a large room with tiled floors and walls even a tiled ceiling with a few lights hanging from it the room was long and quiet thin it had small rooms that where built into the walls from ceiling to floor with a small door on each which stretched from about neck to knee obviously changing cubicles along the wall and a

small walk way to a door obviously leading to the pool there were no windows they both stepped into a cube next to each other so they could talk to each other luckily the way that they were meant neither of them could see anything Luna was finished first she had changed into a small swimming costume and stood in the main area of the room till she put her arms on the top of one of the door of Isaac cubical "hi Isaac" she said making him jump and almost sequel "Luna do you mind" he said going close to the door so she didn't see anything

"No I don't you continue" she laughed

"I can't if you're watching me" he complained

"But I can't see anything you know" she said

"That's not the point I can't change when you're staring at me Luna" he explained

"So I can when you stare at me" she replied

"I don't stare" he replied

"Yes you do Isaac even when you don't think you are, remember the day with the light" she joked

"Of course I do" he replied

"Well what would you call that then" she asked

"Looking often" he replied

"No it's staring Isaac" she laughed

"Okay fine but that doesn't mean you have to do it to me" he pleaded

"what are you getting so worked up about it's not that bad Isaac I mean what am I really gunna see" she laughed

"At the moment a lot" he said bluntly looking down then back to Luna

"Seriously, have you even got anything one behind there" she laughed

"NO I HAVEN'T so if you don't mind Luna go away" he shouted trying to make sure she didn't just look over the door at him

Luna just laughed at him "please Luna" he pleaded

"fine" she said moving so she was out of his view but if

she just moved her head slightly she would have been able to see him but she didn't she just stood there quietly till he came out with not a lot on just a pair of swimming trunks with his arms crossed over his chest looking a bit less nervous then he was last time he stood like that back in the theatre "im good now" he said going to lean and kiss her but she put her finger on his mouth "what are you doing" he said the words slightly slurred by the fact Luna's finger was on his mouth

"We are gunna play game" she laughed

"We are?" his words again slurred

"yes we are Isaac" she said stepping back from him still with her finger over his mouth "no nothing okay Isaac, if you want me you have to catch me" she said before running of Isaac then ran after her quickly catching up to her till they ran right in to the pool room the pool was quiet big but it was quiet dark only the lights where the lights in the pool they both ran all the way around the pool before Isaac caught up to Luna slinging his arms around her waist from behind she kept screaming till he lifted her of the ground and held her over the water and spun her around so she was facing him "that was a mean game Luna" he said

"No it was fun now put me down" she laughed

"Oh I will put you down I guess I will just let you go" he joked

"No put me back on the floor Isaac" she squealed

"Why should I convince me not to just drop you Luna" he laughed

"Isaac stop messing around put me back on the ground" she said

"No I think I should just let go" he laughed

"no" she squealed as Isaac dropped her into the pool she then swam up spitting water from her face as Isaac laughed and sat on the floor so his feet kicked the water

"that was not   very funny Isaac" she said

"No it was hilarious" he laughed

"Shut up Isaac" she said gripping his foot and pulling him into the water with a splash when he got back to the surface he looked at her angrily "I wasn't ready" he said "Of course you wasn't Isaac" she laughed

"Have I caught you now" he said putting his arms around her

"I suppose I don't have a choice" she replied

"No you don't" he replied

Isaac then put his now wet glasses on the side of the pool Luna just looked at him for a second "what" he asked

"Nothing just...looking at you without your glasses" she answered

"And?" he asked with a smirk

"You look better with them Isaac" she laughed

"Thanks Luna you're so nice to me" he said sarcastically

"Your welcome" she laughed

She said pulling him into a kiss that got pretty heated quickly till Luna pulled away

"What was that for Luna?" he asked

"I need a reason" she replied

"Good point" he said

Not much really went on for a while just them both swimming around the large pool till Luna spoke up "hey Isaac I bet you can't jump of the diving board"

Isaac then looked up at the board "you right I can't jump of that" he replied

"Have you tried?" she asked

"No" he answered

"then try now" Luna said getting out the pool so she could sit on the side kicking the water close to where Isaac had put his glasses he then swam over and joined her sitting on the side

"I am not jumping of that" he said

"Fine but jump in from some high I want to test a theory I have" she asked

"What theory?" he asked

"I will tell you when you do it" she laughed

"fine" he sighed he then got up and walked over to the other side of the pool and jumped in and just as Luna had thought a few seconds and what always happens when boy's jump in pools when not high enough there shots come of Luna noticed this and just put her head in her hands giggling till Isaac was in the pool with his arms on the side "Isaac" she giggled

"What now Luna" he asked a bit fed up

"You may want to look down" she said still giggling he did and his face went almost red with embarrassment "did you know that was gunna happen" he asked very angry with her

"Sort of...yes that was my theory" she laughed

"You are evil sometimes" he said

"I know" she laughed

"now keep your eyes shut till I tell you it's okay no peeking al right" he then swam off trying to find his shorts and failing quiet a lot till Luna moved one hand from her face spotting that his shorts where right by her feet and he was looking in the other direction so she scooped them up with her foot and put them on the side with his glasses and continued kicking the water with her face covered "found them yet Isaac?" she giggled

"no I haven't still no looking, I don't understand it's a pool they can't just disappear... okay secondary search eye's still shut Luna im gunna have to get out and look from outside the pool for them" he said he then claim out the pool checking every few seconds Luna still had her hands over her eye's because it was dark in there it was difficult to see and it worked to Luna's advantage as he still couldn't see his shorts where right by Luna

"still not found them Isaac?" she said still laughing but not trying to give herself away as she spoke she moved his shorts behind her and began to stand up "no I can't find them it's ridiculous we will have to leave come back when I have more clothes on" he said jumping back into

the water and swimming over to the side where Luna had been sitting and put his glasses on
Luna still had one hand over her eyes

"You could do that Isaac or you could find them" she said taking her hand away from her eyes and showing him she had his shorts and laughing

"How did you- how did you do that?" he asked very confused
"long story Isaac but if you want them you have to get them" she stepped back just enough to make sure there was no way for him to get them without getting out but still only just be out of reach
"This is not funny Luna give them back" he said
"No I refuse, you want them you have to take them" she laughed
"Please Luna im serious" he begged
"No, no,no,no,no begging will not help you Isaac" she laughed
"Please what do I have to do" he said almost laughing at the ridiculousness of the situation
she then walked back holding his shorts in the air so he couldn't reach then kicked some water at him with her foot she then sat on the side still keeping the shorts out of his reach with her foot on his shoulder so he couldn't come any closer to take them "Luna what do I have to do?" he pleaded
"Information that's all I want off you Isaac" she said sternly
"What information" he asked very worried at this sudden change in her tone of voice from the happy, cute and playful, to anger and impatience
"you know exactly what information Isaac, what is it you think you know about my past or I will leave you in here and hook up the video camera to you tube live constant feed now tell me" all playfulness in her voiced had

vanished and the smile was gone from her face now
replaced with a look of waiting
"okay, what I think I know is that you're not who you say
you are because Luna Redgrave is legally dead and that
your gunna have to run off soon and I- and I will never
see you again" the last part his voiced changed almost
like he was crying
"Is that all?" she asked
"Yes" he answered
"You swear that's all you think you know" she asked
"I swear on the only thing that matters to me" he replied
"Which is?" she asked
"You" he answered
"Isaac listen to me, I am who I say I am why would I lie to
you and that email was junk im not going anywhere for a
long, long time" she said
"You promise" he asked
"Of course I do" she answered
"Okay, can I have my shorts back now?" he asked
"Fine" she said throwing them back to him so they
landed on his face
"No looking Luna" he told her
"Fine" she said putting her hands over her face again
"Done all good" he said as her got out the pool to sit with
Luna she looked unhappy "what's wrong" he asked
"Nothing Isaac" she didn't remove her gaze from the
water when she answered
"No tell me Luna or I will uh....uh.... I will keep you
locked in here forever" he said
"Liar" she replied
"true but what's wrong Luna please tell me" he said
wrapping his arms around her waist she was still facing
away from him so he put his head on her shoulder and
waited for a response
"Nothing's wrong, im just worried" she answered
"What about?" he asked
"That camera" she answered

Chapter 9

Isaac looked up to the camera in the corner of the celling looking almost directly at them "why don't we give him something to look at" he said slyly giving her a kiss on the cheek

"No Isaac not happening" she told him
"Why not Luna, what's stopping you?" he asked slyly
Luna just turned to look at him before shaking him of and jumping in the pool after a long while of the two of them swimming around not doing much till Isaac was sat on the side again and Luna was swimming around "you know Isaac when I was little I used to swim for hours pretending I was a mermaid" she said pulling her arms on the side of the pool with her head just above the water just beside him

"Really I didn't know that Luna" he began to lean into her as he spoke
"yep and I watched a movie once and I remember this happened" she said as she slowly reached up grabbing his face with both hands kissing him then pulling him into the water with her for a long time they just kissed and cuddled in the water till they heard the door open someone else was coming into the pool they both then swam to the side and ducked so however it was couldn't see them both when they looked it was Harrison he stepped into the room in little more than a dressing gown and sat on the side of the pool putting his feet in the water kicking it about "Harrison" Isaac said
"Wow, hey Isaac didn't know you were in here two" Harrison said casually
"Yep been here all day" Luna said
"Oh Luna your here to, please tell me you guys have clothes on" he asked very worried

"Yes we have" Luna snapped

"Now" Isaac added

They both then swam over to where he was sat

"I thought you two were not an item" Harrison said

"That was quite a while ago now" Luna replied

"Really that's really gunna piss Mel off" Harrison laughed

"Why" Isaac asked

"Mel has had her eye on Isaac since our first theatre lesson" Harrison explained

"I know but me and Luna had our eyes on each other from that first day when I crashed into her" Isaac said

"Aww you guys are so cute" Harrison said

"Thanks" Luna said sarcastic

"But I have to ask Luna does he rather sleep with you or his bear" Harrison asked

"Funny story that" Luna began

For quite a while they all just talked and joked about a lot of things till

"well I think I will leave you two to get back to what you were doing before I burst in on you but remember camera, so keep it PG see you guys latter" he said as he left the room leaving Isaac and Luna alone again Isaac then looked at Luna with a suggestive look "what is that look for?" she asked

"I don't know maybe I disagree with Harrison" he said slyly wrapping his arms around her again

"Disagree with what?" she asked

"Us keeping it PG" he then leaned in to kiss her before-

"way wow Isaac slow down a bit, okay save something for the next few years or you will get bored" she said stopping him

"I could never get bored of you Luna" he said

"You say that now" she sighed

"I could never get bored of you Luna you are always so full of surprises to keep me on my toes for a million years let alone five" he explained

"shut up Isaac" she said splashing some water in his face

eventually turning into a splashing war till Isaac swam up and sat on the side with Luna still swimming around a bit "hey Luna" he said getting her attention

"Yes Isaac" she said still swimming

"How far would you let me go? Like back in the room?" he asked carefully

"What?" she said now swimming back over and leaning on the side beside to him

"You know exactly what I mean, how far?" he asked

"I don't know Isaac it depends" she replied

"On what" he asked

"Lots of things" she replied

"PG?" he asked

"Well obviously" she answered

"12?" he asked

"Yeah" she answered

"16?" he asked

"Maybe" she answered

"18?" he asked

"Possibly" she answered

"R?" he asked slyly

Then after a long hesitation "...if your good Isaac" she answered

"Really?" he asked

"....yes" she said

"YES" he shouted incredibly happy

"I said if you're good" she told him

"I will be good I promise" he reassured her

"I know you will Isaac now come on before it gets to late" she said claiming out the pool

"Okay" he said

Luna then got her towel and wrapped it around her Isaac then got up and practically ran around "come on lets go, let's go come on Luna" he kept saying

"Wow, somebody's a bit over existed I said I might let you I never said we were going to Isaac" she told him

"I know that I just want to go back"

Luna just sighed and walked off to the changing cubicles
Luna went in the one she had before so did Isaac but he
didn't start to change he waited abut a minuet before
trying to be quiet and do what Luna did to him and be
nosy he was just returning the favour he put his arms
over the door it was dark he couldn't see much plus she
was facing away from him and quiet close to the door
"hey Luna" he said slyly
She jumped then just glared at him "ha ha very funny
Isaac, do you mind" she said
"No I don't mind at all" he joked
"Very funny Isaac very funny now don't stare" she told
him
"Im not im just looking" he said slyly
"Yes but it's what you're looking at im worried about" she
replied
"I don't know from what I can see I wouldn't be worried"
he laughed
"It's fine im almost done anyway" she sighed
"really?" he backed away from the door before noticing
she had already got her jeans on and she had a bra on
already "dam should have gotten here earlier" he sighed
"Relax Isaac you wouldn't have seen much anyway, as
you're out there save me the trouble go into my bag over
by the wall and get my shirt out for me" she asked
Isaac gave her, her whole bag and she just smiled at him
he then went of to change himself after a few seconds
there was a voice at the door "hey Isaac" she giggled
"hey Luna" he said as he came up close to the door again
so she didn't see anything before making her giggle by
putting his shorts over the door and smirking at her he
then looked around his cubical then at Luna confused
she just stood smirking at him trying not to burst out
laughing "Luna did you by any chance, take something of
mine" he asked
"I don't know Isaac what are you looking for?" she asked
it sounded like an actual question

"You know exactly what im looking for Luna" he said
"Im sure I don't Isaac, what are you looking for exactly?"
she was being honest she didn't know
"Luna you know what im missing now what you have
done with them?" he asked
"Done with what?" she asked
"My boxers" he said
"I haven't touched them I swear" she told him
"Well who else would have took them?" he asked
"I don't know but I didn't steal them I promise" she
reassured him
he then looked around again looking though all his bag
finding no trace of them till he found a small piece of
paper that read in a scribbled handwriting "sorry I hope
you won't mind Isaac but I had to borrow your boxers
will give them back soon from Harrison"
"That arse hole" he said
"Who?" Luna asked
"Harrison has taken them" he replied
"Why?" she asked
"He says he had to borrow them" he answered
"I don't think I want to know why" she said
"Well what am I gunna do now?" he asked
"I don't know but no matter what it is it's gunna be
funny" she giggled
"I can't walk all the way back to the room in just my
jeans" he sighed
"Well I don't see you have much an option" she giggled
"Can't you go to the room and get me another pair" he
asked
"I guess I could, where are they?" she asked
"Bottom of the wardrobe" he answered
"Fine" she sighed
Luna then walked of still giggling to herself all the way
back to the room she put her stuff down on the bed then
went to the wardrobe and got what she assumed where a
clean pair of Isaac's boxes it was difficult to tell with all

his clothes they looked dirty even after you washed them she then walked back to the pool with his boxes in the pocket of her jacket she opened the door to an mysterious silence "Isaac im back" she said as she stepped more into the room she saw the grounds keeper holding Isaac by the arms he was now wrapped with a towel around his waist

"I cause this boy doing something he shouldn't" he said Isaac looked down at the floor almost now glowing red

"She doesn't need to know what I was doing" Isaac said sounding terrified

"I think she does" the grounds keeper said

"PLEASE DON'T" Isaac begged

"Are you his room-mate Miss Redgrave?" the grounds keeper asked

"Yes why" Luna said

"You may wish to keep an eye on him, I caught him.......pleasuring himself" the   grounds keeper told Luna

Luna just looked at Isaac who was still looking at the floor and she just burst out laughing

"I didn't have a choice" Isaac said

"it is against the rules to do such a thing here in this room Mr Richards, you may do such things in England but not here thank you" the grounds keeper said Luna was still laughing hysterical at him, for a second he picked his eyes from the floor looking at Luna but it only made him blush a deeper shade of red then before he wasn't smirking though he looked guilty

"Now Mr Richards you may think I have embarrassed you am I right" the grounds keeper said

"Well yes as a matter of fact" Isaac snapped

"Well im not done with you yet" the grounds keeper said

"What?" Isaac asked

"Mr Richards I think we should tell your room-mate what it was I caught you saying as you did it" the grounds keeper said with a smirk at Isaac

Isaac just looked up to him extreamly scared
"Please I beg you don't" Isaac pleaded
Luna just looked at him she had now stopped laughing
and was stood with her arms crossed looking at him
"One or the other Mr Richards you tell her or I do" the
grounds keeper said
"Please don't, please" Isaac said letting his head fall so
his chin was on his chest staring at the ground
"Last chance Mr Richards" the grounds keeper said
"I was.............I was saying...." Isaac began
"What where you saying Mr Richards" the grounds
keeper asked
"Can we drop it" Isaac asked
"what where you saying Mr Richards the words you kept
repeating" the grounds keeper said tighten his grip on
Isaac arm Luna just kept her eyes on Isaac who was still
staring at the floor
"Please I will tell her latter just not with you around
please" Isaac begged
"fine" the grounds keeper said letting go of Isaac's arms
then walking out Luna didn't remove her gaze for a
second she was still stood arms crossed looking at Isaac
he slowly picked his head up to look at her "so did you
get me some clothes?" Isaac asked
"Yes I did" she said getting the boxers out of her pocket
"Good give them here" he said
"No" she told him
"Why not?" he asked panicking
"What words Isaac?" she asked with a smirk
"No please don't make me im begging you Luna" he said
literal getting to his knees in front of her pleading at her
"No Isaac, no words, no boxers that's the rule" she
giggled
"Please it's embarrassing" he said
"If you don't tell me I will go back to the room and
destroy all your boxers now tell me" she laughed
"No I won't tell you" he said crossing his arms

"Fine I guess I will go destroy all your clothes then go ask the grounds keeper what it was you were saying" she said being to walk away

"No, no, no please" he said pulling her back and keeping hold of her legs so she couldn't go any where

"Tell me Isaac" she said

"fine....I was saying..." he looked around making sure on one was around before getting up looking extreamly annoyed before whispering into Luna's ear "oh yes Luna please"

"What?" she asked

"You heard me" he said extreamly embarrassed

"Really?" she asked

"Yes okay now can we drop it and forget about it" he asked

"No we can't Isaac" she said laughing at him

"Why not?" he asked

"Because I said not" she replied

"Why not Luna?" she asked again

"Because I say so" she said throwing him his boxers he quickly put them back on under the towel "can't we just drop it" he said getting fully dressed

"Obviously you couldn't drop it" she said

"Not funny Luna" he replied putting his jeans on and chucking the towel away before again standing very embarrassed and slightly angry

"Let's go" she said walking out Isaac followed her at a distance

"Luna, are you mad at me?" he said catching up with her

"No Isaac why would I be mad im surprised certainly but im not mad" she replied still walking away

"Really my mum said girls get angry when guys do that" he said

"Some girls do, but what you do when you're on your own is none of my business Isaac and in all honesty im not sure I want to know, but one thing is for certain" she said

"What?" he asked
"You're not holding my hand ever again" she laughed
"Why not?" he asked
"I don't know where your hands have been" she laughed
before running of again he quickly followed her as soon
as he got close enough he wrapped his arms around her
waist and lifted her up and over his shoulder "Isaac put
me down" she said hitting his back and kicking him
repeatedly "no I refuse to put you down" he said
"Why, what have I done" she asked
"You hold sensitive information" he said walking off to
their room

Chapter 10

When they got back Luna was still over his shoulder she
was now bored he sat her on the bed for a moment "am I
gunna be allowed to do as I wish now" she asked

"maybe in a minuet but as for right now im gunna have a
shower" he said he then walked of Luna just laid back on
the bed silently laughing to herself till a little while later
Isaac came back wearing only a towel
"Hey Luna" he said
"Hey Isaac" she replied
"Can I ask you something?" he asked
"Sure shoot Isaac" she replied
"How much did you see?" he asked
"What?" she asked in reply
"How much did you see in the pool?" he asked
"Not much relax Isaac" she giggled
"Liar" he said putting some boxers and his pyjama
bottoms on under his towel before removing it and sitting
down next to Luna and lying back on the bed
"Okay maybe I am lying" she giggled
"How much did you see Luna?" he asked

"All but the main attraction Isaac" she replied
"Really?" he asked
"Yep" she giggled
"I hate you sometimes" he said
"Liar" she giggled
"Exactly" he said sitting beside her putting an arm
around her and giving her a kiss on the cheek
"What exactly where you thinking about while I was
gone?" she asked
"What do you mean?" he asked
Luna just made a suggestive face at him and he realised
what she meant
"Oh ,oh, nothing that important" he said putting both his
hands in his lap and trying to look more at the floor
again
"Really then how did the grounds keeper catch you if it
wasn't important" she laughed
"I was....uh... a bit loud then I maybe should
have....been" he admitted
Luna then just started laughing at him again
"Don't laugh at me Luna" he said
"Why not, it's funny" she laughed
"No it isn't it's horrible to get caught I swear the times
one of my sisters caught me they by the time I was 16 no
one in my house was surprised to see or hear it" he
explained
Luna just continued to laugh at him almost falling of the
bed
"Don't laugh at me, how would you like it if someone
caught you?" he asked

"Girls don't do stuff like that Isaac" she told him
"Really" he asked
"Yeah girls don't do anything like that, well some do none
I don't though, and girls don't have that danger" she
explained
"Really but what if you did how would you like it to be

interrupted before you had finished your... business" he said

"Why is that how he caught you Isaac?" she laughed

"As a matter of fact yes but how would you feel in a similar position" he asked

"What having like having you walk in on me doing something like that screaming something embarrassing" she giggled

"Exactly" he said

"I don't know Isaac" she said

"Okay, what would you be screaming though" he asked

"I don't know just remind me what where you saying" she giggled

"Do I really have to repeat it?" he asked

"Yes you do with correct voice pattern" she asked

"What?" he asked

"Act like you were saying it back then" she giggles

"Oh come on" he sighed

"No if you are gunna do this you have to do it right" she laughs

"Fine it went something along the lines of: OH YES, YES, YES LUNA PLEASE GOD LUNA PLEASE YES, I think anyway" he shouted

"Really that's how you got caught being too loud with that" she asked

"Yep" he said laughing "come on what would you be screaming Luna" he asked

"I don't know something along the lines of: OH ISAAC YES DON'T TEASE ME OF ISAAC I think it might go something like that I would imagine" she said

"Wow, you know I asked about how far I could-" he began to ask

"No Isaac not today" she told him

"What you can't do that than just make me go to sleep that's not fair" he said

"I told you don't bother getting existed but you never listen to me Isaac" she said once again falling back onto the bed looking up at the celling

"It's been a good day you know im happy you suggested that idea this morning" she said

"Im happy I did two it's like out a movie" he joked

"All we need now is a cheesy love song and a slow dance and we have a rom-com" she joked

"that can be arranged" he said as he then got up and put the cheesiest slow movie song he had on and pulled Luna up wrapping his arms around her waist she moved her arms to his neck and shoulders and they both slowly swaying to the music not an inch of gap between them both Luna then nested her head on his chest in response he up his head on the top of hers till the major note of the song like in every movie when every movie couple kisses   they met and kissed till the song was over and Isaac pulled away and looked in her eyes and he said "and roll credits"   marketing them both laugh

"Not yet im not done" she replied pulling him into another deep kiss

"Can I roll credits now" he asked as they pulled away

"I think so anything else will be part of the out-takes" she said

"I don't know maybe it could be an extended scene you only get on certain versions you have to pay extra for" he said slyly

"No I think it would be an out-take" she said

"Why is that" he asked

"Because nothing interesting is gunna happen" she said as she left his arms and got into bed ready to go to sleep

"Aww" he said

"maybe some other day Isaac" she replied as he got into bed next to her putting his arms back around her pulling her close again "no we have to sleep Isaac or else" she said

"Or else what" he asked

"You never get what you want and I will move back to my own bed" she threatened

"You're mean sometimes" he said

"I know it's a gift" she said giving him a peck on the lips before turning away to sleep

"You know a while back we would never have imagined this" he said wrapping his arm around her

"I know we wouldn't if someone here invents a time machine I will go tell back then me not to jump to any conclusions when I meet you" she said

"That would be nice to not be first asked if I was gay" he laughed

Luna then laughed

"Im so sorry I said that Isaac" she said

"I know you are, besides I thought you were a nutter a couple of times" he said

"Thanks and what do you think now" she asked

"I think you're the best girl on earth Luna, what about you what do you think now" he asked

"You're defiantly not gay or just in a really deep cover, night Isaac" she said

"Night Luna" he replied

then like a flash Luna was asleep yet Isaac stayed up a little while longer thinking about what she said in the pool she said she wasn't going anywhere but he didn't believe her somehow it seemed to him like she was just waiting, like him she was savouring every second not quiet getting the power to get up and go just yet but it worried him of that email was right and people where coming after her how long would it be till they got there and what would they do, was making her happy and make her want to stay gunna be the worst choice ever, he then realised the longer she stayed with him the less chance she had of like she said surviving day to day till after a while of thought he finally fell asleep.

Chapter 11

the first awake was Luna she woke up slowly sitting up
slightly when her phone rang luckily it was quiet enough
for it not to wake Isaac it was Julia "hello dear" she said
"Hey Aunt Julia" Luna replied
"I need to talk to you urgently dear" Julia said a bit angry
"Can it wait a little while I will have to shake Isaac of he
follows me round like a puppy sometimes" Luna said
looking over at the sleeping Isaac
"No, no dear bring him with you it involves you both"
Julia answered
"Okay sure we will be there as soon as we can okay bye"
Luna said
she then hung up put her phone back and rubbed her
eyes till Isaac moved in his sleep "so im a puppy now am
I" he said getting up
"Yes you are" Luna replied
"I thought I was a baby" he asked
"Your both a baby and a puppy, you're a baby puppy
that's what you are Isaac" she smiled
"Well woof" he said sarcastically trying to lean into Luna
for a kiss but she just pushed him away

"No we need to get up Julia needs to talk to us urgently"
she said
"Oh god what did we do" he asked
"I don't know....WHAT IF THE GROUNDS KEEPER
SPOKE TO HER YESTERDAY" Luna said in a panic
they both looked at each other put some better clothes
on and ran out the room not even   locking it running
down to Julia's room and knocking on the door franticly
as they waited they noticed Luna was wearing her top
inside out and Isaac had Luna's jeans on and on
backwards it wasn't that noticeable it was just quiet
uncontrollable for him but there was little they could do
about it now at least Isaac had put a shirt on now unlike
earlier when the door opened it was Julia in her classic

yellow dress looking at them both sourly "in here now young lady and you Isaac" she sounded very angry but it didn't really change her voice pitch that much they both stepped in to the grounds keeper sat on a sofa drinking some tea Julia then assorted him out leaving Isaac and Luna standing there looking very nervous Luna grabbed his hand and they both held a tight grip on each other knowing they were both about to be killed for yesterday when Julia came back into the main part of the room and she sat on the sofa looking at them both angrily

"Well care to explain yourselves" Julia said
"Explain what Aunt Julia?" Luna asked
"You know exactly what Luna Redgrave, yesterday in the pool young lady" Julia answered
Isaac couldn't help but snigger till Julia shot him a look

"I don't know what you're laughing about young man you're in more trouble then she is" Julia said
"Why what we do" Isaac asked
"You know exactly what you two did yesterday, at some time or another students will break a rule but you two managed to break several in one day I told you Luna before you came here that you were on no condition to go see the grounds keeper for anything, you are not allowed around campus when it is closed, you went in the pool without a correct regulations specified" Julia explained
"Such as" Isaac asked
"such as the lights on Mr Richards, then you continued to... well you know what you both did all that kissing and messing about with only the fact of the grounds keeper doing what he did to stop you two from going any further" Julia explained
Luna didn't say a word she just looked down at the floor
"What do you have to say for yourselves both of you?"
"Im sorry it won't happen again I mean a lot of what happened was accidents I swear" Isaac said

Luna said nothing

"Well young lady what do you have to say for yourself"
Julia asked Luna

"Im sorry Aunt Julia" Luna said not picking her head up
her voice barely audible

"well at least you to are sorry but im still not happy with
either of you that's why I will be phoning your father
later Luna about what has happened and Isaac I will be
phoning your mother too and I have half a mind to
separate you two" Julia explained

"NO" Luna said raising her voice

"What did you say to me Luna" Julia asked a bit shocked

"I said no Julia im not a baby you can't tell me what to
do any more and neither can dad im an adult you can't
punish me that much because on one mistake I made im
human okay deal with it, you can't rip us apart please"
Luna shouted almost screaming

"I think I may not have a choice Luna you two have
caused no end of trouble since we put you together it
may be for the best for both of you" Julia explained

"no, im sorry but that's not happening even if you chain
me to a wall you can't keep us apart, ask me not to be
with Luna would be to ask me not to breath or not to
think I can try but it just won't work, please you can't do
this to us" Isaac said for once raising his voice pulling
Luna into him so they were hugged together clinging onto
each other like a child to a teddy bear when told to let go
of it they didn't even look at Julia they just looked at
each other with their foreheads pressed together just
staring into each other's eye's till Julia spoke up again

"it's not my decision the head of the collage will decided
when he gets back tomorrow he will evaluate the
situation and it's up to him not me, now get out my sight
both of you" they both then ran out and stood outside
both almost crying

"Im so sorry Luna if I hadn't suggested it this wouldn't be happening" he said

"Don't you dare apologise Isaac it's not your fault it's mine if I wasn't being too silly and childish this wouldn't have happened" she said

"No it's not your fault either Luna, don't you dare say this is your fault" he replied

"It's both our faults maybe people just can't accept that were two big screw ups" she said

"Two screw ups together cause a lot of damage" he replied

"I know but no matter what happens tomorrow I will always love you Isaac no matter what they do to us" she said

"no matter what even if my mother takes me home and makes me marry Melissa I will find my way back to again they can't keep us apart forever, I love you Luna" he replied

at that second the door to Julia's room swung open with her stood almost crying "that was the most beautiful thing I have ever heard, I haven't heard something that beautiful since your mother passed away Luna, your so much like her you know more than you think you are I will try my best to put in a good word for you two to try to keep you together or just lesson the sentence I don't know but I will try I promise" Julia said

"thank you" they both said before running off back to their room both almost crying when they got back they both just sat or hours in each other's arms doing nothing but sitting together in sweet silence both crying "I don't what to lose you Isaac" she said

"you won't I swear no matter what they do to me I will come back to you I won't even think of anything else it may take me seconds it may take me year's but I promise I won't leave you." he said

"I won't leave you Isaac I promise they would have to kill me before I give in and let you go, but if something does

happen this may be our last night together" she said
"It won't be I promise" he said
"but what if it is there is so much to say so much to do
and time is against us" she replied
"I don't know" he said
"Isaac if it was our last day together what would we do"
she asked
"Sit here and never let go Luna" he answered
they both then sat back on the bed and laid side by side
still holding on to each other not even an inch apart just
holding on to each other refusing to let go they didn't
sleep that night they didn't want to waste the time they
had together asleep till around six am Julia walked into
their room she looked very sad almost crying "we need to
go see the head of campus, im so sorry" she said Luna
and Isaac just got up slowly still holding onto each other
till they got to a long corridor with a door and a small
chair outside where Julia left them they just stood
together looking into each other's tear draw eye's till a
man in a black suit asked to see Luna they told Isaac to
sit and wait she gave him a kiss goodbye before stepping
into the room it was a large room with not a lot in it but
a large window a desk and two chairs the man sat in one
facing with the window behind him he told her then to sit
in the other seat she did nothing but look down trying to
hide the tears in her eye's

"so miss Redgrave, I am full aware of the rules you have
broken you and Mr Richards and normally when these
rules are broken in this manner we often have to expel
the students or transfer them at consent from parents to
completely different collages miles apart" he explained

 Luna then began to cry again

"but in this situation I have decided to be slightly kind
miss Redgrave it is clear to me from the footage of the

two of you and the account of yesterday from your aunt that there is a real connection there and as much as it pains me to say it but it was in some respects the collages fault if we hadn't put you two together this may never have happened that's why you will be staying here and Mr Richards will have a slightly more appropriate punishment" he explained

"No please you can't split us up please im begging you please" she begged

"It is the rules miss Redgrave" he said bluntly seeming to have no care for Luna's feelings at all

"no please you split us up and I will leave to and if you send me away he will come after me we made that clear yesterday we will not be pulled apart" she explained

"I am well aware of that miss Redgrave you will be staying in your aunts room till further notice you things should have already been moved by the campus security im sorry" he said

he then told her to leave as she stepped out the door campus security let her out and Isaac in at the same time so there was no way of constant they then told her to wait outside and wait.

As Isaac went into the room he was told to sit in the chair he didn't say a word at first

"Mr Richards now I believe you know the rules for this situation" Isaac just nodded in response "often in this situation the girl stays here and the boy will be transferred somewhere else do you understand that" he just nodded again not really looking at him "but I feel in this situation that would be extreamly cruel, to both of you it has become apparent to me though the footage and accounts and from miss Redgrave it would be just cruel to do that to you both but punishment is in order the two of you will be separated on campus till further notice and new rules in placed banning this sort of activity outside of your shared room again if it happens again then I will not hesitate to move you both out of this collage and into two collages thousands of miles apart do you understand" Isaac again just nodded in response "Speak up Mr Richards" he said

"thank you sir" Isaac said quietly he looked happy yet still so sad by the time he got out Luna was gone moved off somewhere he didn't know where he guessed that was the idea so they couldn't talk to each other and lean where each of them was going to be he went back to the room no matter how he looked at the room it seemed empty all Luna's belongings where gone everything he just sat on his bed for a while looking up at the celling he did nothing for days on end just sat on his bed curled up crying his eye's out ready to give anything for a man to tell him he could see Luna again UN fortunately they had now installed a camera outside his room so no matter what they both did the grounds keeper would know about it quite a few times he wanted to step outside and swear relentlessly at it but he didn't he just sat crying for day's

much like Luna when they took her away from the door she was left with boxes and bags in her aunts room she would have to sleep on the sofa but she didn't really sleep she just sat around on the sofa staring at her phone she wasn't even aloud to send him a message they blocked the numbers on their phones so they couldn't talk to each other Julia would often be talking but Luna wouldn't be listening she was to in her head thinking about Isaac all the memories she had of him no matter what they were good or bad from the tiny little arguments to the best of kisses even that simple crash when they meet seemed like the best thing on earth to her this went on for as long as both of them could remember all thought the holiday's till a few day's into the new term both Isaac and Luna didn't go to lessons they were separated rooms now so they didn't bother going when Jake got back alone no girl he stepped into the room expecting to see Isaac and Luna sat cuddled together but no he only saw Isaac passed out on the floor by his bed surrounded by bottles he'd been drinking when Jake got him up and sat with him on the bed "what the hell have I missed Isaac" Jake asked

Isaac just sat looking at the ground till he finally spoke the stench of the alcohol still in his breath and he began to cry

"We broke a rule or two and they separated us I know she's somewhere on campus I just can't see her I can't talk to her they even blocked our phones so that we can't message each other and cut off our internet access so we can't email" Isaac explained

"Oh my god for how long" Jake asked

"Until further notice but that was almost two months ago Jake I don't know how much more I can take of this before I lose it" Isaac explained

"It is okay man you will be fine im sure they won't keep you apart much longer before they realise the effect it is having on you both" Jake said

"It's all my fault if I had just let her do nothing like she wanted this would never have happened" Isaac said sadly

"Relax man it will be okay I know it will you and Luna would survive the apocalypse trust me you will both be fine im sure" Jake said with a smile

Chapter 12

Meanwhile Luna still with Julia only ever moved from the sofa when she needed the bathroom and her eye's never moved from her phone on the table till Julia came to sit with her a while

"Luna you really must do something dear you can't sit around all day everyday" Julia said to Luna

"I will do something, when I can see Isaac" she answered briefly

"then good news dear end of the week you will be allowed to return to your room with Isaac you will be of time table for a while as you get back into order and such so Friday dear you can see Isaac on Friday" Julia explained
"Really?" Luna asked
"Really" Julia answered
"Thank you Julia" Luna said
"Come on help me clear up a bit from your living here miss" Julia said
For the first time in what seemed like years Luna began a small smile.
Isaac learned the news a day later as men began to pack boxes back into the room he rushed around going at a million miles an hour making the room look spotless not really a difficult task on Thursday night Isaac got Jake to sit and talk with him a while "so when are you meant to see her" Jake asked
"I don't know" Isaac answered
"Where are you gunna meet" Jake asked
"I don't know" Isaac repeated
"What are you gunna wear" Jake asked
"I don't know that either" Isaac said
"Well why not use my phone to send her a message to make your reunion special and memorable" Jake said
"Like where we first meet where I crashed into her" Isaac suggested
"Perfect man I will send her the details and make sure it's special Isaac or she will never forgive you" Jake said
"I know Jake" Isaac sighed
when Jake sent the message Isaac decided on fashion not really much of a decision he was gunna wear jeans and two shirts he didn't have anything different he probably washed around 12 timed that night before going to sleep when he woke up he showed again took a lot of time to style his hair but it still looked ordinary when he was changed Jake came to collect him and walked with him to the spot he meet Luna it was still quiet early

"So how exactly did you two meet" Jake asked
"well she was lost and so was I, she was looking at her map standing right there I was trying to run around and follow the map and crash I ran into her making us both fall to the ground after looking at where we needed to go we found we were roommates" Isaac   explained
"Sweet, positively cute" Jake laughed
"Thanks" Isaac sighed
"Okay my plan I told her involves you facing that way" Jake pointed to the other direction he told Luna to arrive in but that was his idea to do the whole big reveal idea from movies
when Luna revived the message on Thursday evening she showered for a very extremal long time and picked her clothes for once she was gunna be different a bit daring with her fashion she put on jeans and a dress over the top it was a white dress that normal would have been knee length and a small jacket as she left on Friday morning she couldn't not smile even though people she passed probably thought she was crazy till she got to the spot Jake told her to go to see could just see Jake he told her to stand in a certain spot and cover her eyes till he shouted in the message so she did at that second he shouted then turned Isaac around they were close enough to see and hear each other "Luna" Isaac said happily
"Isaac" Luna said happily
"Please don't tell me you're a hallucination" Isaac said
"I will if you do" Luna replied
they both laughed before quickly walking to meet in the middle in   a huge embrace basically crying into each other for a while till they noticed people began to crowed around them wondering what was going on but they both just ignored them "I missed you so much" Luna said
"You wouldn't believe how much I missed you" he replied
They then both ran of hand in hand back to the room

and locked the door they both sat calmly on the bed for a second just looking at each other holding hands till Luna spoke "so how did you do without me?"

"Pretty bad. What about you?" Isaac asked

"I hardly moved for two months Isaac" she answered

"I sat crying for most of it" he sighed

"Aww, that's so cute" she said

"No it isn't its pitiful Luna I sat crying" he sighed sounding a bit upset and annoyed about it

"No it's cute I missed you so much Isaac" she said hugging him

"I missed you two trust me my average shower time must have tripled I swear" he said

"Aww, Isaac you really did miss me" she said pulling him into her more so they were only a few inches apart

"I must warn you im a bit out of practice Luna I haven't done this since you've been gone" he told her

"I know neither have I" she replied

they both pulled into an extreamly hot passionate kiss that only got deeper per second his arms went to cradle her waist her arms went up his chest and around his neck before both of them still kissing fell backwards onto the bed still passionately kissing till much latter Isaac moved his hands down slightly from her waist towards the top of her jeans when Luna stopped him

"Okay that's enough of that for tonight"

"What no please" he said in a panic

"I said no not tonight" she told him

"You said that last time though" he sighed

"I know and im saying it again" she told him

"please Luna do I have to beg like a puppy" he said as he sat up on the bed crossed legged looking at her attempting puppy dog eye's at her having no effect she just laughed at him "Aww Isaac your so cute sometimes"

"Why am I not cute all the time" he asked

"I didn't say that, you're just extra cute sometimes" she then sat up and gave him a kiss he of course tried to

make it go a bit furtherer but Luna just pulled away
again crossing her arms and glaring at him "im sorry
Luna it just two months is a long time without a girl
around I just got a bit existed" he explained
"Isaac calm down okay don't try and do everything at
once we have six days of time table to get sorted out and
im sure we will have some time to kill then" she said
putting her hand on his leg she just smirked at her hand
then looked up at the celling biting his bottom lip before
he spoke "okay" he answered his face instantly regretted
saying it as Luna got up and went into the bathroom for
a shower and Isaac immediately went out for a cig when
he got out there he noticed Jake standing on his balcony
"hey man, where's Luna?" Jake asked
"Shower" Isaac answered
"Right so how's stuff going" Jake said smirking and
making a extreamly suggestive face
"What do you mean Jake" Isaac asked carefully
"You know, boy, girl two months apart and you come out
for a cig alone either you have pissed her of or..." Jake
said as he made the suggestive face again
"No, we are not like that" Isaac said
"Or is it that she won't let you" Jake asked
"Oh who am I kidding you am read me like a book Jake,
yep im not allowed" Isaac asked
Jake just laughed at him
"What's so funny" Isaac asked
"It's just the way you put it you're not allowed" Jake said
laughing
"Yep don't you think I have tried on more than one
occasion" Isaac sighed
"Whatever but can I ask you something?" Jake asked
"Shoot Jake" Isaac sighed
"What exactly did you two do to get that punishment"
Jake asked
"Oh, right I never told you, a long trail of accidents
mainly" Isaac answered

"Well tell me the story" Jake said

Isaac then recounted almost all of what Jake had missed while he was gone almost everything he did skip the talk he and Luna had about the screaming though when he was done Jake just stood thinking till he finally spoke "wow, that is just wow I did not expect you or Luna to be that... how to explain it but to be that adventures and impulsive"

"Your telling me it's like a whole new side to both of us I never noticed but I think I like it Jake" Isaac said happily

"Cool I guess but you got to be care full or you will make a move you will regret" Jake said to Isaac

"Jake" a familiar voice called seductively from inside Jakes room

"What love" Jake shouted back

"Who are you talking two" the voice asked

"Just a mate of mine" Jake answered

"Really?" the voice asked

Suddenly when he looked Isaac could see Mel wearing not much more than underwear at the door of Jake's room "hey love" Jake said slyly to her

"What you doing out here so late, I want you in there" she said hardly noticing Isaac was there

"I know baby but I just had to talk to Isaac about something" Jake explained

"Are you done now" she asked

"I think im good Isaac any last second thing's" Jake asked

"No you guys get back to whatever you were doing" Isaac answered

"see you soon man" Jake said before walking into his room after Mel and shutting the door Isaac just looked around a moment before going back inside to see Luna wrapped in a towel brushing her hair "hey Isaac what was all that about" she asked

"Nothing just Jake and his new room girl" he answered

"Who is it now" she asked

"Mel" he answered

"Really, we'll all to their own I guess" she sighed

"That's not very nice Luna" he told her

"Well I don't have to be nice to Jake do I? He's not my boyfriend is he?" she asked

"no he isn't and he never will be" Isaac said locking the balcony door and shutting the curtains then he sat next to Luna watching her brush her still soaking wet hair till he moved to me laid on the bed facing up with his head dangling off the end

"Luna?" he asked

"Yes Isaac" she replied

"Did you know something?" he asked

"That depends to what you are referring" she said concentrating more on brushing her hair then whatever Isaac was talking about

"Did you know? Mel calls Jake like a dog like if she wants him she will just call and he is expected to come running." Isaac explained

"Well of course, Mel is that sort of girl" she said

"Are you that sort of girl?" he asked a bit worried making sure to look directly at here even if to him she was upside down

"What do you mean Isaac?" she asked in reply

"I mean would you do that" he said sitting up normally

"No why would you think that?" she asked

"Well you do call me an animal" he sighed

"I call you a puppy because you are a puppy, your cute you always follow me around ,you have big brown eyes and you always make me smile" she said lazily wrapping her arms around his neck giving im a Eskimo kiss

"Aww" he replied wrapping his arms around her waist

"Exactly so stop complaining so much" she said pulling away and playfully hitting him on the chest

"Im not complaining" he replied

"Yes you are Isaac" she giggled

"Okay maybe I am but we need to get some sleep so

hurry up" he told her

"Why do we have something to do tomorrow?" she asked

"Yes, well I do" he answered

"What do you have to do tomorrow?" she asked

"I have to go into town for something" he answered

"For what Isaac?" she asked

"Nothing you need to know it's a surprise" he answered

"Why can't I know now?" she asked

"No you have to wait till tomorrow to find out" he told her

"Your mean sometimes" she sighed

"Im just returning the favour" he replied

Luna gave him a playful hit to which he fell on the bed acting like he had been shot till Luna got dressed under the towel and got into bed Isaac just sat on the edge of the bed for a while looking at her "what?" she asked

"It's just good to see you back in that bed after this long" he said and they both smiled

he then got changed and sat up in bed with Luna for a while they both stared at each other's cuddled together in the dark "I missed you Luna" he said

"I missed you two Isaac" she replied

Chapter 13

when Luna woke Isaac had already gone he left her a note but no idea where he was going when she had showered and got dressed she put most of her stuff that had been moved from one room to the other back in its original place in the room then sat on the bed with her script from theatre she had now learnt most of it but she still had to read over the lengthy scenes every now and again to make sure she did know it till it was getting to mid-day and there was still no sign of Isaac till much later that day around 3pm by now Luna was sat on her computer she heard the door open and close "im back" he said

"Where have you been?" she asked

"Somewhere now shut your eye's for part one of the surprise" he told her

"okay" Luna said cautiously before shutting her eye's she felt the bed move like someone was sitting on it "okay you can open then now" when Luna opened her eye's she could see clearly his huge black glasses where gone "im not sure I like it Isaac" she said

"It's official I don't need them anymore, unless im using the computer expressively, what do you think" he asked

"I don't know, it's different but I will get used to it" she sighed

"Thanks' Luna" he said sarcastically

"You look fine Isaac" she replied giving him a kiss "what's the other part of the surprise?" she asked

"Oh yes, one there is a party on campus at one of the big dorms we are not invited" he answered

"So?" she asked

"So we are gunna follow an explicate plan I have made" he told her

"Okay, what is this plan?" she asked

"we are gunna lock the door and let no one in or out, we are gunna sit and watch horror movies till we get to scared to blink, we are gunna have loads of junk food I have bought and I swear on my life here and now that I will not try to make a move tonight" he explained

"Sounds like a good plan" she answered

Isaac then moved on the bed so they were sat up against the head board with lots of pillows and around a million blankets cuddled together with the curtains to the balcony shut so it was quiet dark only the table light was currently on "so what in the line of junk food do we have Isaac?" she asked

"we have popcorn, gummy sweet's, chocolate there is ice cream in the freezer, we have crisps and something special" he then pulled out from behind the bed a bottle of Luna's favourite drink she didn't much like alcohol it was a nice alternative she almost snacked it out of his hand "I love you" she said more to the bottle

"Where you talking to me or the bottle?" he asked

"I was talking to you my tall, beautiful golden friend" she said to the bottle

"Hey your talking to the bottle, aren't you?" he said

Luna then returned to how see originally was and unscrewing the bottle

They then put on the movie to them it wasn't very scary didn't really frighten either of them at all they didn't say anything till the credits where on the screen "explain to me why we bothered to watch that?" Luna asked

"I remember that being much scarier the last time I watched it" Isaac replied

"Okay what's next?" Luna asked

"Uh....next is this one" he told her

"Oh okay" she said

they then watched horror after horror movie each one getting scarier as the night went on both of them getting closer together as the night went on with every jump scare till at one movie they were both sat cuddled together with blankets up by their faces a jump scare and they both screamed making they both almost break the bed as they both jumped up terrified of the thing on the screen till the credits began to run "we are not watching that one again" Luna said

"Im never answering a phone call again" Isaac replied

"Good idea" she said

at that second the phone rings making them both jump again into each other's arms Luna looked at the phone ringing she reached out to get it "don't it could be the dead" he whispered

"It says it's my aunt" she whispered back

"Same difference" he replied pulling Luna closer to him

"But it could be important" she said still scared

"But it could be your call Luna" he told her in a hushed whisper

The phone then rang of making her phone come up with the words one missed call they both just sat together terrified till on the other side of the bed Isaac's phone rang making them both scream again

"It's say's it's your aunt again" Isaac whispered like the phone could hear him

"Maybe it's a cover for the dead" she replied

"Im not answering it" he said

"Im not answering it" she replied

when the phone rang of his screen now also said one missed call they both moved to they were in the exact centre space between the two phones "what movie is next before they ring again" she said as a clap of thunder came from outside "uh I think the last on is horror house" he told her

"No, no,no,no,no,no,no" Luna complained

"What why not" he asked

"I refuse to watch that movie" she told him

"Why?" he asked

"Because not okay" she said

"Come on Luna we have watch almost every horror film I know why not this one" he asked her

"because Isaac I lived with older brothers so I watched Horror Housewhen I was five you don't know what that does to you, I hate that movie" she explained

"Really but it's okay we know it's all fake and im here aren't, I will keep you safe" he said to her

"Please Isaac can't we watch something else" she asked

"No we are gunna watch Horror HouseLuna" he told her

"Please Isaac I will watch anything else but that" she said

"No Luna im standing by this we are watching this movie" he told her

he then shifted on the bed so he was sat on the end changing the DVD Luna moved behind him putting her hands on his chest and kissing his neck "come in Isaac

im sure we could find something else to do" she said slyly
he simply turned his head to look at her he pulled a face
of amusement at her "is that your best argument Luna
come on you can do better than that" he said still sorting
out the DVD to play she groaned in annoyance "please
Isaac I will happily watch anything else but that" she
begged
"No Luna we are watching this" he told her almost
ignoring her now
"Please" she asked
"No" he said
Luna then began to moved her hands down his chest
towards his pants
"No Luna it's not happening try again" he said
"Please Isaac" she begged
"I said no Luna" he said moving her hands away from the
top his jeans
she then sat and thought for a moment Isaac was still
sat on the edge of the bed till Luna moved so she was sat
on his lap blocking his view of the TV running her hands
up and down his chest "come on Isaac you really can't
think of anything better to do than watch some silly
movie" she whispered slyly in his ear at this point Isaac
was struggling to cope with the temptation of what she
was doing till he moved his arms around her waist but
twisted so she fell on the bed "we are watching the movie
then you can do what you want" he told her
"Come on Isaac I really don't what to watch this" she said
"Okay if you get to scared I will turn it off I promise" he
said sitting back at the head board of the bed with Luna
she looked very angry at him
"Fine" she said sighing
"come here" he replied he up his arm around her and
pulled her close taking her hand she put her head on his
chest as the movie began as it went on Luna kept
tightening her grip on his hand but overall as it went on
Isaac was more scared then she was not to say there

wasn't a lot of screams from them both went it was
finished "we are never watching that again" he said in
fear
"I warned you Isaac" she sighed
"Im never sleeping again" he said in fear
"You can't stay awake for ever trust me I tried" she told
him
just then there was a knock at the door that terrified
them both with another clap of thunder with it they
looked at each other wondering if they should answer it
till there was an even louder knock at the door it
sounded as if someone was punching the door but not
making another sound, they both sat looking at the time
it was around 3am who would want to see them both at
this time of day they began to hear a strange sound
almost like someone picking the lock and they both
heard the door swing open and the light from outside
they could see a large shadow of a man in the door but
there was no sound till a man stepped in dressed in
black with his face covered he looked at them then got a
knife Isaac and Luna just started scramming holding on
to each other till the man walked over to their bed knife
still in hand and he spoke "are you Harrison?" the man
asked looking at Isaac
"What?" Isaac said still petrified
"Is your name Harrison?" he repeated
"No im Isaac who the hell are you?" Isaac said in fear
The man removed the material covering his face it was a
man a little older than them with a five a clock shadow
he looked dirty
"Im James, im looking for Harrison, he has a debt to pay"
he man said
"Uh we don't know where Harrison is" Isaac said
"Who are you?" the man asked
"Im Isaac Richards" Isaac answered
"Im Elizabeth Richards" Luna said
Isaac then looked at her strangely

"Brother and sister?" the man asked

"No married" she replied

Isaac then looked at Luna trying to not look gob smacked but it was difficult till the man left shutting the door and they could hear the man was gone "what the hell Luna" he asked

"What do you mean?" she asked pretending not to know what he was talking about

"What was all that about" he asked

"Just something okay don't ask about it" she told him

"No I think I need to ask Luna, what they hell did you do that for?" he said getting up and standing by the bed looking very confused

"Isaac you don't need to know please just-" she began

"No im not falling for it this time Luna what they hell did you do that for" he asked

Luna stayed silent for a while

"TELL ME LUNA" he shouted it was strange Isaac didn't get angry very often but she still didn't say a word

"Luna please just tell me why a maniac has come through our door at 3 in the morning with a knife and you give him a fake name what the hell is going on" he asked

"I can't tell you Isaac" she said

He stood thinking for a minute before speaking "if you loved me you would tell me Luna"

she looked up at him with tears in her eye's wiping them away she told from him to sit with her and she got her laptop pulling up the email again scrolling down to the sentence at the end "the boys are after me Danny's boys are after me I lied to survive, Isaac now can we drop it" she explained

"Why are they after you?" he asked

"I don't know, they have been after me for as long as I can remember even when I was back with my family been running ever since" she said as she then started to cry he pulled her close so she was crying on his shoulder "oh

my god Luna im sorry, I shouldn't have asked im sorry
you can use my last name all you like you can pretend to
be my wife all you like" he told her
When she finally stopped crying she moved away from
him to sit with her head on her knees and arms folded
looking away out the window away from Isaac
"Why would he have been looking for Harrison" Isaac
asked
"I don't know maybe he did something" Luna replied
"Like what" he asked
"I don't know Isaac but im sure we will find out" she
sighed
"Okay at least I know something but what if Harrison
tells him something and he comes back" he asked
"I don't know" she replied
that night they both went into a deep sleep worricd that
at any second someone was gunna march in and kill
them till it was morning Luna woke up first they had to
be back to classes tomorrow so they didn't have much of
a plan so she made breakfast and set the table even
though it was closer to lunch time she sat down and
began to eat her food like normal when Isaac finally got
up he sat up or more jumped up looked around the room
franticly then calmed down before noticing Luna wasn't
next to him he began to panic before realising she was
sat up the table he then walked over and stood beside
her before giving her a kiss and stealing a bit of toast
from her before returning to being sat on the bed "so
what are we gunna do today" he asked with his mouth
full
"I don't know" she replied
"You don't know much recently do you Luna" he joked
"No I don't Isaac, currently more important things on my
mind" she replied
"Like last night" he asked taking another bite from his
toast
"Not exactly" she said

"Then what exactly" he asked

"Nothing that important just trivial stuff" she said

"Like?" he asked

"Like...if it's possible to get a hangover from sheer" she replied holding her head

The both laughed for a bit

"Maybe that's what we could do today experiment on if that's possible" he laughed

"No, we need to do something today" she said

"What do we need to do today?" Isaac asked

"Try and fit in some practice of theatre before tomorrow as we haven't done it in like two months" she replied

"Good point but can I ask you something" he asked

She looked up at him concerned before answering

"Sure shoot Isaac" she said sounding distracted

"Question one to practice theatre do I have to get dressed" he asked

"I don't think so not unless you plan to do anything else today" she answered

"Okay, question two, Are you going anywhere?" he asked

"What do you mean" she asked

"You know exactly what you mean now they found Harrison are you gunna have to run of" he asked sounding very sad

"No" she answered

"are you sure I mean how long till they work out you lied and come get you Luna are you positive because if you're not then do go and leave me here as soon as possible" he said almost crying "all I mean is that it will destroy me either way you could just get it over with that's all" he was now crying looking down at the floor Luna moved so she was sat with him on the bed she hugged him tightly till he began to stop crying before pulling away just enough to see his face

"Isaac I told you before im staying here" she told him

"But stuffs different now you have to leave to keep yourself safe, surviving day to day Luna" he told her

"Isaac I swear to you im not going anywhere im stay here with you" she said

"If you stay with me you'll die" he told her

"No I won't I will be fine, trust me for once Isaac trust me" she told him

"okay" he replied hugging her tightly again he didn't notice but she did look rather worried now when they had both calmed down and the day almost seemed normal for a little while till latter that day an idea popped in Isaac's head

"Luna" he said from the other bed they now used as a stuff place where he was sat on his laptop

"Yes Isaac" she said back from the kitchen area just finishing loading the dishwasher

"You know well quite a while ago you said how far I would uh be allowed to go" he asked

"Yes" she sighed

"And after what uh....happened last night" he made a very suggestive face at her she just crossed her arms and leaned against the wall in the kitchen area

"Get to the point Isaac" she told him

"Is the rule I put on last night about the no moves not on today?" he asked

"It was on for last night making it void since this morning Isaac" she told him

"Right, then one more question" he said

"What?" she sighed now a bit bored just wanting him to get the point

"Am I allowed to uh... you know" he again made the suggestive face Luna just laughed at him

"You think you have to ask for permission?" she said

"Wait I don't" he said in surprise

"No" she told him

"YES" he said getting up and wrapping his arms around her leaning in to start kissing her

"Hey, wow... wait a minute, we are not doing this now" she said trying to get him off her

"What but you just said-" he began

"I know what I just said the fact is in your current state no" she told him

"What state?" he asked

"For one you desperately need a shower, actually yeah have a shower and I will think about it" she told him

"Promise you will think about it" he asked

"I promise" she said

"Fine" he sighed as he walked to the bathroom she did have a point he did need a shower after a quick smell of his clothes he did agree with her.

Chapter 14

After he showered he put some clothes on just the standard fashion he all way's wore he went back into the room to see Luna sat on the bed watching some TV he went and sat with her gave her a kiss then said "am I suitable for you know my lady"

"Maybe" she laughed

"Thanks" he said sarcastically

"Your welcome Isaac" she sighed

they then both sat watching TV for a while before there was another knock at the door they both looked at each other Luna gave him a kiss then she ran off into the bathroom to hide, he opened the door to see Mel standing there in a pair of blue shorts and a bright pink top her blonde hair sat on her shoulders

 "I need a word with you Isaac" she said

"Sure I guess" he sighed

She then stepped inside and stood around in the main part of the room

"So I see your room-mate Luna is out how long is she gunna be" she asked slyly

"Uh I don't know" Isaac replied

"Good, I heard a funny story from Jake you know" she giggled

"Really what was that then" he asked leaning on the wall not paying much attention to her

"Well two really one I heard you're a virgin" she giggled

"Yeah why" he asked

"It's funny that's all, and I heard Luna won't let you get rid of it" she replied slyly

"Oh, no ....not exactly-" Isaac began

"So you have lost it" she asked

"No I still have it" Isaac replied not too happy about it

"Oh... okay" she said as she looked at him while biting her lip

"Shouldn't you be getting back to Jake, Mel" Isaac asked

"he's gone out to see his friends and Luna's out so maybe we can fix both our problems then" she said trying to step closer to him

"I don't have any problems" he said with a nervous laugh as he backed away from her

"Yes you do, you're a virgin and alone and im a girl who's boyfriends is out we can solve our problems together" she said slyly to him

At that second Luna had had enough of listening to this and came out the bathroom making it look like she had just got back from somewhere

"Uh... LUNA" he said noticing she was there

"Hey Isaac" Luna said slyly as she stood beside him and then kissed him passionately just generally to piss Mel of a little more "hey Mel, what are you doing here" Luna asked

"just talking to Isaac Luna , see you guy's tomorrow" Mel said then walked out looking very annoyed when they were sure she was back in Jake's room Luna backed away from him crossed her arms and looked at him

"What I didn't do anything" he said

"I know you didn't you were thinking about it though"

she said
"No I wasn't" he answered
"Liar" she relied
"No for once im not lying about this I wasn't thinking about anything I don't think of Mel as anything more than Jake's girl I wouldn't do that to you" he explained
"I know you wouldn't, you don't have the brains to make it work" she answered
"HEY" he complained
"Sorry" she replied sitting on the bed in her usual place
"Now what where we talking about before all that" he asked slyly sitting beside her
"you know I don't remember" Luna said
"You know exactly what we were talking about Luna" he said leaning in to kiss her but she just put her hand over his mouth
"Not now Isaac maybe latter" she said tuning the TV on to another channel
"But it is latter" he complained sitting on his knee's looking at her with the puppy eye's again she just laughed at him
"Really seriously you're obsessed with this" she replied
He just nodded in response
"Come on Luna please" he said giving her the puppy eye's again and pushing out his bottom lip looking like a baby
"Aww you so cute when you beg for stuff you're not gunna get" she giggled
"I give up, I will have to be a virgin forever" he said moving so he could sit crossed legged on the bed facing the TV putting his arm on his leg to hold his head up and look out the balcony window
"What are you doing Isaac" she asked
"Im pouting" he replied briefly
"Aww" she said hugging him from behind putting a kiss on his cheek he looked slightly happier then he returned to looking sad for a while Luna then went off to have a shower he was still sat thinking for a while till she came

back drying her hair with a towel by now he had moved slightly so he was sat on the end of the bed feet on the floor leaning on his arms "you've moved" she said upon entering the room

"My legs went to sleep" he answered

"Well if something of you is tired you should go to sleep" she told him

"No I've been busy" he replied briefly

"What busy pouting?" she asked with a laugh

"No busy thinking" he answered

"What you been thinking about?" she asked

"Just something" he replied with a shrug

Luna then put the towel in the wash and sat on the bed beside him but a bit further back

"What you been thinking about Isaac?" she asked he looked at her sadly then spoke "im sorry, it's just that pool got me all excited then we were separated im just happy to have you back and I don't know im over thinking everything I guess" he explained

"Isaac relax for once stop thinking about everything so much for once just don't think" she said again hugging him from behind putting her head on his shoulder "maybe you are just over thinking everything" she said slightly moving her hands down his chest he didn't really notice till her hands where a few centimetres from the top of his jeans he was still sat leaning on his arm but slowly removed his head from his arm sitting up a bit more smiling he didn't turn to look at her though he was slightly disappointed when her hands went over his jeans and down his legs "Luna, what are you doing" he whispered

"Im thinking" she whispered back slyly

"Oh, what are you thinking about Luna" he whispered slyly too

"Lots of thing's, why what are you thinking about" she asked slyly

"a billion things right now" he blurted out as Luna moved

her hands back up his leg's her hands never left the fabric of his jeans till she got her hands back to his chest but this time going under his shirt staying in contact to his skin Luna could hear his breath flinching almost every time she moved her hands it made her smirk but he was smiling like mad till she removed her hands from him he turned around very annoyed she just laughed at him and smirked

"I said calm down Isaac" she said tapping his nose with her finger and then pulling him into an extreamly hot kiss them both pulling each other closer till Luna began to lean back but Isaac didn't stop so they just fell backwards on the bed still kissing passionately till Luna stopped him from going any furtherer by pulling away and getting up of the bed

"wait no that's not fair you can't do that then walk away" Isaac said sounding really annoyed obviously tired of Luna's teasing she stood now just of the bed and smirking at Isaac as he crossed his arms and moved back to pouting again on the edge of the bed Luna laughed "who say's im walking away" see said walk to the balcony and locked the door and shutting the curtains before walking passed him locking the main door and dropping the key's on the desk before sitting on his lap making him look extreamly happy again before Luna started to kiss him again running her hands up and down his chest till he decided to start kissing her neck

"Isaac, Isaac cut it out a minuet" she said moving away slightly

"What, what did I do" he asked worried he had messed something up already

"Nothing just do you know what you're doing like really do you" she wasn't joking it was a serious question did he actually know?

"Luna I have had at least one sister going through her teen life at any given point I think I've heard enough of what to do though the thin wall's, what about you do you

know what you're doing" he asked as he two was being
serious
"Isaac I've been on the internet since I was thirteen I
think I've read enough fan-fic's by desperate fan girls to
know what im doing" they then returned to kissing the
next few hours are extreamly self-explanatory a mess of
heat, sweat, flying items of clothing and loud screaming
and shouting till,

Chapter 15
till the next morning they both now laid half asleep in
each other's arms love bites covering both of their necks
Isaac even in his sleep looked extreamly happy his hair
was messy now all out of its usual place, his chest was
exposed and the rest of him covered only by a small
sheet he was facing the ceiling with his arms around
Luna who was laying slightly beside and slightly over him
she like him had nothing on but was wrapped up in the
sheet when the alarm went off Luna got her phone and
turned the alarm off then started to wake Isaac up
"Isaac, get up , Isaac, Isaac" she said hitting his chest till
he woke up
"Morning Luna" he said yawning
"Morning, we have to get up and get to class" she said
stretching
"Can't we skip today go in tomorrow" he pleaded
"No we can't, we have been missing classes for ages im
sick of not doing anything" she complained
"I don't know, I wouldn't say last night we were doing
anything" he said slyly with a smirk trying to reach up to
kiss her neck
"Shut up Isaac" she replied hitting him so he returned to
the bed
"I don't know, you didn't last night did you" he smirked
walking his fingers up her arm
"Isaac you don't just say stuff like that" she said sitting
up and getting some clean underwear and putting it on

she then stood up looking for more clean clothes while
Isaac just laid in bed his head propped up by his arm
looking at her get dressed "don't stare" she told him
"I don't know, I think I should stare you certainly did" he
smirked
"ISAAC" she shouted
"Sorry" he said holding up his hands in defence "I just
pray to god Mel and Jake didn't hear us" he added
"So what if they did we can hear them, and we both know
it would annoy the hell out of Mel" she giggled
"I know but you know Mel if she heard us she's gunna
tell everyone" he sighed
"I know she will but at least it gets it in her head to back
the hell off" she said
they both laughed then Isaac got up and put some
clothes on when they were both dressed they sat on the
bed for a minuet they were quiet early this morning as
neither of them could be bothered to shower this
morning they sat there thinking for a moment before
Luna spoke
"You should cover that up you know" she said pointing to
the mark on his neck Luna's marks where missing she
had covered them with make up
"No im gunna leave it" he smirked
"Why?" she asked
"So that I can for once walk with my head held high
about something im not a virgin any more" he said
happily
"You're meant to cover them up so people don't think
about what has happened" she told him
"Well im gunna use it to piss Mel of a bit more" he
smirked
they both laughed again before getting there stuff and
walking across to the theatre hand in hand people where
already there some girls where rehearsing a dance
number in the production on the stage they both sat
right near the back away from everyone else so they

could sit and chat without everybody listening in after a while Harrison came to talk to them he sat just in the row of seats in front of them and turned to face them "morning guy's welcome back to class after your separation" he said

"Thanks' Harrison" Luna replied

"Wow, Isaac I see something important" he said pointing to the mark on Isaac's neck

"I told you" Luna said to Isaac

"Okay yep its obvious isn't it" Isaac said with a shrug

"Yeah it really is man you should do something about it" he told him

"I know but currently it's working the job I want it to do" Isaac replied looking over at Mel who was sat looking at them angrily Harrison looked over and laughed

"Nice idea mate" he said "Luna can I have a quick word about the thing?" he asked

"It's okay Isaac known's" she answered

"What how much does he know?" he asked

"Most of it not everything" she said

"Up to what?" he asked

"1200" she told him

"Okay, right" he said back

"you guys do understand im right here I can hear all of this" Isaac interrupted

"Does he know about 1200 alert?" Harrison asked

"No and not a word" Luna told him

"Okay can I have some explanation please" Isaac interrupted again

"sure name's Andy, Andy James currently Harrison running from drug gang of Danny zero im a dirty double crosser running for my life, luckily I was able to fool them with a fake name and fake story as I was hooking up with a person I lied to down the pub when he found me and my room-mate was out" he explained leaving Luna UN surprised and Isaac confused

"Good but soon they will be sending Markus you know that right Markus will find you in a heartbeat you need to 1200 like now" she told him

"Im good for a while but as soon as this production is over I will be 1200ing don't worry, what about you how did you shake James?" he asked

"Told him me and Isaac where married and gave myself a fake name didn't suspect a thing helped we were a bit busy with a horror movie marathon at the time" she smiled

"Nice Luna, talk to you guy's latter" he said he then got up and walked off to talk to Mel

"Well that sounded like gibberish to me" Isaac said putting his arm around Luna and pulling her into one side of him

"It is just something nothing important, nothing to worry about" she told him

"Okay, but is there something going on or has there ever been?" he asked her

Chapter 16

"no Isaac I meet him after I meet you him running from the same person is a coincidence trust me, besides he's gay" she answered

"What?" he asked very surprised

"He's gay Isaac" she told him

"wow" he said and looked at Andy recalling everything he knew about the guy "I see that now" he said after thinking a while

they both then laughed and then sat in each other's arms as the other people came and went for different dance numbers on the stage the teacher may not have even notice they were there when the bell rang for the end of the day they hadn't done much work it was mainly dancers working today so they mainly sat at the back of the theatre cuddling and kissing when they knew Mel was watching and sometimes when she wasn't when they

returned to their room they tied up a bit some stuff had
been knocked over and clothes thrown everywhere in the
heat of last night it did take a while just as they were
finishing Isaac spoke "Luna?"
"Yes Isaac" she replied fixing there bed
"Where are my boxers from last night I can't find them
anywhere?" he asked her as he looked around the room
"I don't know I was busy at the time" she said briefly
"oh yes you were" he said slyly putting his arms around
her from behind and pulling her close to him making her
giggle at him "but it's odd like they vanished" he sighed
she then shrugged so he then went and turned the light
on to look for them a bit easier went he noticed a bit of
the light wasn't a bright as the rest he walked over to the
balcony door before noticing somehow he managed to get
them between the light and the celling "Luna" he said
"What?" she asked
"Found them" he said pointing to above the light
She then went and stood next to him and laughed
"How did you get them up there?" she asked
"Im not sure" he shrugged
"But how could you have been on the bed yet got them
there it seems like an impossible shot if you were aiming
that would have been really accurate" she laughed
"Cool im an accurate underwear thrower now how we
gunna get them down" he asked her
"we will have to stand on the bed and get them" she told
him they both them moved Luna sat on the bed as Isaac
stood at the end reaching up on the top of the light when
he found them he just threw them onto the bed beside
Luna "wait" she said picking them up "duck" Isaac then
moved he knew what she was gunna try to do she was
gunna try and make that shot she threw and missed by a
mile "done now?" He asked her
"Fine I don't know how you did that" she sighed
"im not sure how I did that" he said standing up on the
bed again noticing something else was up there it was

small and what seemed like metal when he got it out it
was the Horror House DVD "Luna what's this doing up
here" he asked her
"It's....uh......um........magic" she stuttered clearly lying to
him
"Luna where you trying to hide it so we don't watch it
again" he asked her
"Maybe" she replied
"nice idea but no we will watch this again at some point"
she told her before getting down on the bed and
returning the DVD to its box on the self before sitting
back on the bed with Luna cuddling her "so what are we
gunna do tonight" he said in a sly tone making his
suggestive face again
"No Isaac we did that yesterday" she told him
"That doesn't mean we can't do it today" he replied
"I said no Isaac, you're certainly persistent I will give you
that but I have some work to do" she said
"What work?" he asked
"a theory I have that need's testing" she said before
getting and getting her chair it was an office chair on
wheel's she put it in the centre of the room then sat on it
backwards and sat crossed legged so she was touching
nothing but the chair and she tried bobbing up and
down and moving around on it before letting out a sigh
"what are you doing Luna" Isaac asked very confused but
slightly laughing at her
"I want to know if I can move my chair without touching
anything but the chair" Luna replied
"Why?" he asked
"Curiosity Isaac" she said
"It just looks like your bored and out of idea's" she
replied
"Pretty much" she shrugged
"Well if im honest there is not much to do other than the
obvious options I don't see much to do" he sighed
"We could have another film marathon" she suggested

"What this time?" he asked
"Not horror but something fun" she smiled
they both then went to the shelf's looking at movies not
finding anything they wanted to watch "you know
between us we must have over a hundred movies plus
the internet, and we still can't find anything to watch" he
sighed
"I know we need to do something and there is nothing to
do here" she sighed
"But if we are bored no how are the next few year's
gunna be" he asked
"torcher im sure" Luna said sitting back on the bed and
sighing Isaac then joined her pulling her close to him
"Thinking of torcher" he said making his suggestive face
again just making Luna laugh at him
"You have that stuff on your brain Isaac" she laughed
"Well what do you expect" he asked
"I expect you to talk about something else for once" she
said playfully hitting his shoulder
"But not much has gone on other than that" he told her
"Well stop thinking about it" she replied
"I can't it's engraved on my mind" he complained
"Well try" she told him
At that moment there was a knock at the door
"Well that's an incentive" he said sarcastically
Luna went to the door and opened it,

Chapter 17
It was Jake looking very annoyed
"Hey Luna I need a word with you two" he told them
"Sure" she replied letting him in
He stepped in and stood in the centre of the room by the
chair Luna had been messing around with Luna returned
to the bed where she sat with Isaac he instantly put his
arm back around her
"So there are quite a few bits I what to talk to you guys
about" he said

"Sure shoot man" Isaac said

"First are you aware that I next door can hear you guy's" he asked them

"Yes we know that, we can hear you" Luna replied

"how much do you guy's hear?" he asked a bit concerned

"Most of it im not gunna lie she has got to learn to shut up" Isaac said

"I know, anyway can you please keep an eye of Mel when she's in theatre please" he asked them

"Why?" Luna asked in reply

"She comes home late every time she has theatre and she won't tell me why im curious is all" he answered

"Sure but im not sure it will be difficult to keep an eye on her she mainly watches us like a hawk" Isaac said

"Anything else" Luna added

"Yes, can I stay with you guy's a bit I left my key's in there when I left with Mel so im now locked out till she gets back" he asked them

"Sure make you at home" Isaac said

Jake then went and sat on the chair Luna was on earlier spinning around not really doing much Luna was looking at the TV trying to find something to watch having no success giving up she just rested her head on Isaac's shoulder more and her arm on his chest so he gave her head a kiss in response and held her a bit tighter

"You guys are adorable" Jake said looking at them

"We try" Isaac shrugged

"You know sometimes I wonder if I didn't drop my spider tank and lost her would you two have been at this point by now" he asked

"Who knows but I do think for certain that if you had just chucked me out all those nights we defiantly wouldn't have done what we have" Isaac said

"im the match maker obviously, I don't get it though you listened to my advice and look how happy you guys are and no matter what I do by a few weeks who ever im with either im sick of them or their sick of me" Jake said

"Well try and go for a different sort of girl Jake" Luna said
"Nice idea" Isaac added
"Instead of going for girls like angel and Mel go for a different sort of girl" Luna added
"Well it's an idea for sure" Jake replied
At that moment they heard a knock at the door when Luna opened the door it was Mel looking very angry
"Where the hell is Jake?" she said stepping in the room basically pushing Luna out the way
"Here Mel" Jake said raising his hand
"What the hell Jake what are you doing in here?" she said
"Talking to my friends Mel relax" he answered
"No way am I gunna relax, don't you dare do that now back to our room now Jake" she ordered
"You're not my mother Mel you can't just order me around" he replied
"Why the hell not you are my boyfriend" she said sternly
"So that doesn't mean you can treat me like your pet" he told her
"And why not you are" she replied
Luna and Isaac just sat on their bed trying not to get involved just trying to stay out the way of the argument without it being obvious that's what they were trying to do till Jake said
"This is ridiculous, Isaac you agree with me right" Jake shouted
"Oh....uh.....I don't know im staying out of this" he said in response
"Seriously Luna you agree with me right" Mel said
"We are staying out of this it doesn't involve us" Luna answered
Jake and Mel then left to their own room but it didn't make much difference they could still hear every word of what they were saying but they both tried not to listen but it was quiet hard when they may as well been arguing in front of them again by now it was around nine

at night Luna was sat up in bed reading a book they had their music on but they could still hear Mel and Jake arguing "when are they gunna shut up" Luna said
"God only known's" Isaac replied as he sat down next to her "what are you reading?" he asked childishly looking over her shoulder
"Im reading the hobbit again" she replied
"How many times have you read that now?" he asked her
"I stopped counting" she smiled
"Well stop reading time for bed Luna" he said taking the book out her hand and put it on the table

"Okay" she replied taking her glasses of and rubbing her eye's

 "while you sort yourself out im gunna have a shower" Isaac said before getting of the bed and walked off to the bathroom as soon as Isaac was gone she got her glasses back and continued to read but it was proving to be difficult to focus on reading as the whole room filled with sound Luna either listened to Mel and Jake arguing next door or Isaac's attempting to sing walking on sunshine in the shower after a while she gave up trying to read and went into the bathroom to brush her teeth she stepped in quietly the room was full of steam the mirror covered in condensation, at this point he had stopped singing and the only sound was the sound of the shower running Luna walked up to the mirror and wiped the condensation from it making it slightly clear so she could see herself she really was nothing special in her opinion she started brushing her teeth and just stood there like there was nothing wrong for some reason it was eerily quiet till Luna started to hear a strange sound it sounded a bit like the creaking she thought but it was unlikely till she realise what it was "Isaac" she said quietly

"Luna WHAT THE HELL ARE YOU DOING IN HERE" he

squealed

"I think a better question is, what are you doing in there?" she giggled

"you-uh you don't need to know Luna" he stuttered

"I think I do Isaac" she said just starting to move the curtain but Isaac quickly pulled it back and kept hold of it

"Isaac it's obvious what you're doing in there at no other point do you make that noise" she laughed crossing her arms

"That doesn't mean you need to call attention to that fact" he said poking his head out of one side of the shower curtain

"okay just saying is all, are you sure you uh don't want some help with that" she said for once making the suggestive   face at him he just looked her up and down and smirked

"well if you put it that way" he said indicating with his finger for her to come into the shower and the expected followed suit after that day life very much became a pattern of the same sort of thing for what seemed like months as time went on the only thing on Isaac's mind was Luna and how long till that gang was gunna come after her and try to kill her, it was the last Friday before spring break Isaac and Luna just got back from the theatre "that was ridiculous" he said falling backwards onto the bed

"I agree" Luna replied collapsing beside him

"I can't believe that lecturer, he's annoying I mean we have done that scene over one hundred times" he sighed

"I know it's not even our fault it's Mel she keep's messing it up, at one point I think she was doing it on purpose" Luna complained

"I agree, I mean the scene considers of basically I enter Mel enters she flirts you walk in and over, I don't see what it is she keep's getting wrong" he complied in response

"I know, what does she actually have to do?" she asked

"She has to walk in talk to me hugs me then goes to kiss me then you enter" he answered

"What did she try to do one time" she asked

"She tried to put her hand down my pants" he sighed

"I need a word with her about that" she said unhappily

"And it happened more than once about ten times I think" he said rather annoyed

"Im gunna kill when next I see her" she replied

"I may be a part of the killing" he added

"The more a merrier im sure" she replied

They both then laughed and sat up

"So what are we gunna do tonight" Isaac asked

"I don't know, can we do nothing" she asked

"Well is there anything to do" he asked in reply

"No, we have no plans for the break so nothing to do, want a cig?" she suggested

"Sure why the hell not" he answered

They both then got up Isaac with his arm around Luna they went on to the balcony to see as usual Jake stood with a cig in his hand

"Hey guys haven't see you in age's" he said

"I know we've been...busy" Isaac said a little slyly more to Luna then to Jake

"Trust me I know I can hear you, Isaac you really got to learn to be quieter" Jake told him

"I keep telling him that Jake" Luna said

Jake and Luna then laughed Isaac didn't though he just stood and pouted like a baby

"You know man im still not good with you two being all cute" Jake sighed

"Whatever, so how's the new room thing going?"

"Pretty good" Jake then turned and shouted into the door of his room "it's Isaac and Luna" and Harrison came out.

Chapter 18

"Hey guy's I feel so sorry Isaac about Mel today" Andy said
"You have no idea how annoyed I am at her for that" Isaac said
Harrison or Andy and Jake and been sharing a room for a while as Harrison took Luna's old bed that was just taking up space in there room they went like a couple it's just that Harrison old roommate got a girlfriend living in that room and Mel moved out to god known's where they all didn't really care where she went they just cared she was gone
"So what are you guy's doing for spring break" Luna asked
"We are going on that trip the collage is running to Florida, what about you guy's" Jake asked
"We are going nowhere and doing nothing" Luna said
"Why the collage is running trips all over plus you have your bike Isaac why not goes off somewhere" Harrison asked
"Nah not our style we will stay here" Isaac replied
"Okay but I don't want any unexpected news when I get back this time when we get back I expect to be seeing you guy's cuddled together happy as ever not separated for doing something you shouldn't" Jake told them
"We know Jake, that's never gunna happen again" Isaac said
"And I don't want to hear of any problems" Harrison said making a face at them
"What do you mean?" Luna asked
"I mean in short, I don't want to come back to find in a few mouths there's gunna three of you in that room" Harrison said to them
Isaac just stood a bit confused Luna looked worried at the point Harrison had just made
"well I guess by that face Luna you haven't been checking, but I guess we will see you guy's latter" Jake said as him and Harrison went back into their room

Luna then practically ran back into the room Isaac then
ran after her but she just jumped on the bed
"What the hell was that about" Isaac asked
"They have a point Isaac you need to learn to be quieter
were lucky are bed is on his side of the room and we
don't have people that side or they would constantly be
complaining" she told him
"It's not my fault" he said
"Yes it is Isaac you enjoy yourself to much" she told him
"There is such a thing?" he asked very confused
"Yes when it's possible the people both upstairs and
under can hear you screaming and shouting" she said
"Fine I will try I promise it's just difficult to remember in
the circumstances" he said sitting on the bed beside her
putting his arm around her pulling her close
"Luna?" he asked
"Yes Isaac" she sighed
"What would you think about what Harrison said?" he
asked her
"What do you mean?" she asked in response
"Three in here" he said
"What like a room-mate?" she asked
"No like a... you know, offspring"
"No" she snapped in reply
"That was a quick" he said
"Well I hate kids" she told him
"But if it was ours it would be different" he said
"I said no, no way are we ever having kid's if I have
anything to say about it" she told him
"What if you don't have anything to say about if it just
happens like by accident?" he asked her
"I don't care I will still put up a fight besides you're doing
stuff all out of order kids are like last before you die if we
are gunna do this we are gunna do everything in the
right order" she said
"I know I meant like years from now Luna" he told her
"I know but a long time away if ever okay, that satisfy

your curiosity?" she asked

"For now" she answered

"Good now I need some sleep" she said

"Why are we gunna do anything tomorrow?" he asked

"With you around I never know I have to be prepared" she gigged

they both just laughed as Isaac leaned into to give her a kiss it as usual got extreamly hot till strangely Isaac pulled away "I will be back in a bit I need a shower an less I don't know you want to join me" he said suggestively

"Not today Isaac" she sighed

"Okay back in a bit" he said giving her a kiss on the cheek before going off to the bathroom.

Luna just did like normal and got her laptop sitting on the bed and did nothing of any importance till after quite a while later Isaac came back wearing nothing more than a towel wrapped around his waist as normal he just put his boxers and pyjama pants on under the towel and sat next to Luna on the bed looking over her shoulder to her laptop screen she was on a little game which made him calm down considerably

"Hey Luna" he said slyly as normal

"Hey Isaac" she replied

"What you doing?" he asked her

"Cards, why worried Isaac?" she asked him

"Im all ways worried just more than usual sometimes" he explained

"Yeah when you go into massive panic's" she laughed

"Good point still we have a whole of spring break to fill with god only knows" he said

"I know, any ideas?" she asked

"A few" he replied slyly hugging her from behind

"do you ever think maybe we do that to much?" she asked him

"There is such thing as to much?" he asked in shock turning her to face him

"Yes there is Isaac" she told him
"I disagree" he said slyly pulling her closer so they went an inch apart
"I know you do that's not the point not today Isaac" she replied pulling his hands of her Isaac just laid back on the bed looking at the celling
"What are we doing for dinner today?" Isaac asked lying beside her
"No idea for once you can cook Isaac I can't be asked" Luna answered
"But I don't know how to" he told her
"It's not difficult Isaac make simple food" she told him
"Like?" he asked
"like I don't know get some stuff out the freezer and get some chips from the freezer and use the fryer to fry them it's not rocket science" she explained
"I will try but don't complain when it all messes up" he told her
he then got up and made a laughable attempt at making food it was like watching someone try to fail at it even though he wasn't trying in a lot of respect's Luna did wonder how intelligent he exactly was if she had to guess it wouldn't be that high when he had finished his attempt at cooking it was barely edible as they sat eating it at the table they both couldn't stop laughing Luna wasn't sure what he did but the food was horrible the chips weren't really chips more like plastic and the chicken he had fried was burnt on the outside then the inside was either like rubber or still frozen "what did you do Isaac?" she asked laughing
"I don't know I did like you said and I failed" he sighed
"I don't understand it how to you destroy food this bad" she laughed
"I don't know I just did okay" he sighed
"I just don't understand how you did it" she laughed
they both laughed for a while till Luna cooked much better food and they ate that before getting into bed to

watch more TV after a few hours they were both half
asleep Isaac much more asleep then Luna after a while
Luna woke up slightly noticing the TV was still on she
got the remote and turned it off by now Isaac seemed
completely asleep or at least seemed it to Luna she then
got up and went to the balcony it wasn't even midnight
yet on the balcony next was Harrison stood enjoying the
twilight "hey Luna" he said not turning to her
"Hey Andy" she said
"How's stuff?" he asked
"Okay I guess" she sighed
"They don't sound okay Luna" he replied
"I know they don't im just....terrified" she said
"Of Danny?" he asked
"Yep" she answered
"Well you know what you have to do Luna you have to
1'200" he told her
"I know I do I just don't want to" she said beginning to
cry she leaned on the pole crying into her hands
"Because of Isaac?" he asked
"Exactly Andy" she said still crying
"Well you knew this was coming Luna you knew the first
time you met him you where gunna have to run off at
some point" he told her
"I know I just didn't think it would have to be so soon I
thought it would be age's if ever I had to run, and I- I
never imagined I would fall in love" she explained
"Luna but your just fiction" he said
"No im not Andy" she answered
"What are you talking about Luna you created yourself"
he told her
"No I didn't this is me the real me, I thought by now they
would be looking for a girl under a false identity not
hiding under my own" she explained
"Plain sight" he realized
"Exactly" she answered
"But surely this has happened before Luna"

"no, I have never been like this with anyone before cover or not   I travel alone and stay alone for other's safety but now I don't know what to do, I can't leave him he will chase after me no matter how far I go he will go looking for me that's likely to get him killed but I can't take him with me if I do they will identify him in a heat beat and then we will both be dead, what am I meant to do Andy?" she explained
"I don't know Luna, well do you love him?" he asked
"Of course I do" she said
"Then take him with you, if he loves you two he will stand by you no matter what" he said
"But they will identify him he's not a blend into crowd person" she explained
"Then change him like you change you, make him fake like all those other times when you would change your hair and face and clothes" he told her
"I don't know I just don't know" she sighed
"Well I may have left by the time you make up your mind" he sighed
"When are you going" she asked
"im going on the trip to Florida im not coming back again I know I said I would wait till after the performance but I had a notice from 24 Markus is coming did you get it" he asked her
"Yep I got it from 24 and one from 78" she answered
"78 what did he have to say for himself" he asked
"He said we want you back even though you have decreased in value" she sighed
"Harsh" he sighed
"Yep" she answered
"What are you gunna do Luna" he asked her
"I don't know any more, I really don't but im gunna know by the end of spring break for definite" she answered
"Sure" he said
"Good luck Andy, hope I meet you on the right side of town next we meet" she said

"Good luck to you to Luna I hope you don't regret whatever choice you make" he told her
"I hope I don't either" she sighed
he then left going back into him and Jake's room leaving Luna still stood thinking for a very long while till she began to cry again just so unsure of what to do till later that morning Isaac stepped out onto the balcony rubbing his eye's then the rest of his face before crossing his arms over his uncovered chest "it's cold out here" he said

Chapter 19
"I know it is but I needed to think" she replied
"Think about what" Isaac asked
"Just something" she shrugged
Isaac leaned with his back on the pole looking at Luna extreamly carefully up and down multiply times
"well not cig so, not worry, no look of anger ,no apparent injury's I can see ,still not dressed, phone hast been touched neither has laptop , your pissed at something ?" he said
Luna shook her head
"Are you re-thinking life?" he suggested
Luna just shook her head again
"You had another message?" he suggested
Luna just shook her head again not bothering to look at Isaac she was lying that time but he didn't need to know about the message from 78 it would only make him feel worse about the situation
"Are you thinking about spring break?" he suggested
Luna didn't reply at all
"Are you angry at me?" he asked
Luna gave no sign at all she was too deep in her thoughts
"Are you dumping me?" he asked
Luna looked at him at exactly the wrong moment as he said that to see his eyes almost full of tears
"Please I can fix what I did please don't dump me, please"

he said franticly jumping to the floor of the balcony on his knee's begging her before wrapping his arms around her leg's

"Isaac im not dumping you" Luna said finally saying something

"You're not" he said getting back up of the floor and returning to his original position

"No I couldn't Isaac" Luna said Turing so that her back was on the pole beside Isaac

"okay....... then I don't-" he began his face suddenly full of fear his hand went to his mouth failing to cover his open mouth expression hitting himself in the face in the process he looked differed as he turned to face Luna

"please tell me it's not what I think it is" he said franticly his eye's glare directly at her's

"That depends what do you think it is" Luna said trying to remain calm and not give herself away

"please god tell me you're not" he began as he put his hands around her waist but then moved them back so they were resting on her stomach his glaze now shifting between her eye's and her stomach

"NO, no Isaac im not chill" she said pulling his arms of her and turning back to face out of the balcony he then calmed down slightly before wrapping his arms around her waist from behind and resting his head on her shoulder

"Well then tell me I can work it out" he said

"It's nothing Isaac" she replied

"When you say that it usually is something" he said

"Well today it's really nothing" she answered

"I don't believe you" he told her

"You never believe me" she sighed

Isaac then griped her tightly and spun her around so she was facing him

"come on Luna you can tell me anything" he said connecting there forehead's together but he kept his eyes shut till Luna began to cry again Isaac opened his eyes and pulled away far enough to see her eye's they were full of tear's "they found Harrison they are sending Markus and he will be here in a few day's Harrison is 1'200ing" she cried

"And why aren't you packing your bag's Luna?" he asked her sadly

"Because im not going anywhere" she answered still crying

"ow Luna, oh yes you are, your gunna run of leave any trace behind you run of somewhere they will never find you I can't watch some nutter kill you Luna I can't do it" Isaac replied now also crying

"No im staying here with you" she said

"No you're going Luna even if I have to throw you out this room you're going before it gets too late" he told her

"Isaac im staying with you" she told him

After a long hesitation and them both calming down considerably Isaac spoke

"Okay fine but if anything happens then I will never forgive you" he said giving her a kiss before pulling her back into the room "so what are we gunna do today" Isaac asked

"Nothing" Luna replied

"Why is that all way's your answer?" he laughed

"I like nothing" she said

"No, no nothing for once we need to do something" he told her

"Well, what do you want to do?" Luna said sitting on the bed

Isaac then sat next to her

"You already know the answer to that" he said as he began to kiss her neck "no Isaac enough not today" Luna replied

"Fine then what do you want to do" he said giving in and stopping

"I want to have a chat -" she began

"What sort of chat?" he interrupted sounding very worried

"A chat about Mel" she continued

"What about her?" he asked

"She's gunna make some sort of move in the next few day's im sure and when she does I expect something of you" she said

"I know Luna, I am expected to stand up for myself and keep my hand's to myself" he said

"No quite the opposite" she said

"WHAT" he snapped now extreamly confused

"what I mean is I expect you to do what you've been wanting to do for ages and just go with it I mean it's not like you have any option soon" she explained

"Luna I don't care if you go a billion miles away I will not go anywhere near anyone else till either you come back or I find you" he told her

"What if I don't ever come back" she suggested

"Then I will find you" he answered

"What if you don't find me" she asked

"I will, there are only so many places you can go on this earth" he said as he began to kiss her neck again

"Isaac cut it out" she told him hitting him

"No I refuse" he said between kisses

"I said cut it out, or else" she said pushing him of her

"or else what?" he asked

"Or else I will never let you touch me again" she threatened

"Fine" he replied now very annoyed "then what are we gunna do we have a month and nothing to do in it" he sighed

"I don't know im sure we will find something, besides put some clothes on" she told him

"Why are we going somewhere nice?" he asked

"Well we are gunna go and see the guys of as this will be the last time we will probably see Andy" she answered

"Why?" he asked

"The trip is also working as his 1'200" she explained
"Good idea I guess it gets him far away fast" he said
they both then got dressed and headed down to the main
part of campus where lots of people were getting picked
up in car's and lot's where boarding buses and coaches
to all sorts of places when they walked around hand in
hand a lot of people gave them strange look's but they
both didn't think much of it what made them both a little
happier was that they sore Mel on a coach to the
California coast they almost hoped she wasn't coming
back after a few seconds Jake and Harrison spotted them
and came over to them Harrison gave Luna a hug before
looking at Isaac out of earshot of Jake "I guess you guys
know this is it" he said
"Good luck Andy" Isaac said
"good luck both of you" he replied before getting onto the
coach then Jake gave them both a smile and a wave
goodbye as he bored the coach to they all waved goodbye
as the coach drove off into the distance down the road
after a while of wondering around campus watching as
the last few trips went of leaving not many people still
there only a few people scattered around the whole
campus, when they returned to their room Luna sat on
the bed using her laptop while Isaac was in the shower
after a few minutes Isaac got out the shower and went
only in his towel and sat with Luna
"Hey Luna?" Isaac said
"Hey Isaac" she replied
"So what are we gunna do for the rest of this break?" he
asked
"I have no idea" she answered
"Well what do you want to do?" he asked
"I don't know, what do you want to do?" she asked
"Uh.............I don't know either" he sighed
"im sure we will think of something" Luna said packing
away her laptop for quite a while nothing really happened
just what they would normally do just gaming and

watching TV this went on for a few day's till Isaac spoke up "im bored"

"So am I" Luna replied turning the TV off "well what else are we gunna do?" she asked "we could go into town" she suggested

"Nah nothing fun in town" he sighed

"We could.................have another movie marathon" she suggested

"We should do that tomorrow and watch every movie we have then we know we are wasting time" he suggested

"Okay we begin the world's biggest marathon tomorrow what are we gunna do today" she asked "what about going to sleep for a while" she said

"Nice idea" Isaac said wrapping his arms around Luna and trying to kiss her neck

"Not that sort of sleeping Isaac actual sleeping with dreams and such" she told him

"Oh not the other one" he said a tad disappointed

"No" she told him

"Nah can't be asked to sleep" he said still not letting go of Luna

"How about going for a walk in the park across the road" she suggested

"why not" Isaac replied getting up of the bed and standing around Luna then got up and found her jacket they both then walked out the room locking the door and headed out they walked across campus hand in hand hardly anyone was around when they got to the park across the road they turned around and looked at the balcony of their room they knew it was these because they left a light on as they wondered around they wondered why they hadn't come here before it was a beautiful place with lots of high tree's and beautiful flowers around with lots of paths in all different directs they both didn't leave each other's grip no matter what happened there were no other people after a while they could clearly see the stars come out it made the hole

place even prettier in the starlight they walked for a long
time just talking about nothing of any importance till
they walked down a path to a dead end with a bench at it
they sat on it looking back at the rest of the park Isaac
put his arm around Luna pulling her close and kissed
the top of her head
"We are so rom-coms sometimes" Luna said giggling
slightly
"And what's wrong with that?" he asked
"Nothing's wrong with that im just saying" she sighed
"We are like a movie couple sometimes but then we know
we are gunna have a happy ending" he told her
Luna just laughed for a while till she got up "come on
time to go back or we will get locked out" she said
"I know" Isaac said also getting up and taking her hand
again as they walked back to the room when they did
they both just changed and got into bed Isaac as normal
wrapped his arms around Luna pulling her close he
began to kiss her neck getting no response other than a
elbow in the chest which made them both laugh but he
still kept his arm around her more than anything he just
wanted to know she was still there and she hadn't left he
was now very unsure on whether or not she was lying
about leaving had she actually give up on running to be
with him or was it just a lie to try and keep him happy
and with that last though they both fell into a deep sleep.
The next day they both woke up and stretched "so movie
marathon today" Isaac said
"Yep we better get started or we will never get finished"
she sighed
so they did they didn't even get changed they just sat up
in bed with the curtains shut and the lights off watching
movie after movie everything they had of every genre from
rom-com to fantasy to sci-fi to mystery everything and
after two day's straight of movies snack foods and
cuddling Isaac spoke up
he turned to movie to pause and sat up he rubbed his

eyes then spoke "Luna we have to sleep we have been watching movies for 48 hours straight I need sleep to function and we haven't even made a dent in the movie pile" he explained yawning

"I know this will take us forever to watch all of these but I don't have any other idea's" she yawned in response

"How about we go to sleep and see what we want to do when we get up" he suggested

"okay" Luna said putting her head on her pillow and almost fell instantly asleep, Isaac then just let his body fall back onto the bed and also fell straight asleep.

first to wake up almost another 48 hours later was Luna she sat up gave Isaac a poke he was still fast asleep so she got up and made herself a crumpet she sat on the bed eating it while reading her book for a bit was nice and quiet till suddenly almost like he had heard a noise Isaac sat up in almost full conciseness he was breathing deeply his eye's wide sweat running down his face it almost sounded as he sat up like he screamed

"Isaac, you alright?" Luna asked him

Chapter 20

He turned to look at her before retuning his gaze front on he was still breathing rapidly "bad dream" he blurted out between his breaths

"What was it about you look petrified?" she asked him

"Nothing important" he said calming down slightly

"Are you sure it dam looked important Isaac, come on you all way's make me tell you everything now it's your turn" she ordered crossing her arms

Isaac turned to look at her "I thought someone had come back last night why we were both deep asleep and they took you away" he then began to cry putting his head in his hands

"oh Isaac, look, look im still here and im not going anywhere relax" she said removing his hands from his face and wiping away a few stray tears on his face and pulling him close to her so his head was resting on her shoulder he had now almost stopped crying he wrapped his arms around her again not wanting to let go till Luna finally pulled him away from her so she could look straight into his eye's "Isaac I told you im not going anywhere" she said

"I know I just worry is all" she said childishly

"I know you do, that's why your my little baby puppy" she smiled

"Aww, I love you sometimes" he smiled giving her a kiss

"So you don't love me all the time" she pouted

"No, just more than usual sometimes" he joked

they both laughed and kissed as usual it turned very hot very quickly till Luna pulled away "maybe later Isaac not now" she said

"What why not?" he asked a bit annoyed

"Because you haven't showered in almost a week go be clean or else" she told him

"fine" he said giving her another kiss before he got up and went to the shower Luna just laughed again before getting changed into some normal clothes and going for a cig on the balcony after a while Isaac came and stood with her in his jeans without a shirt quiet a usual thing now "am I clean now" he said sarcastically

"As clean as you're ever gunna get Isaac" she said also sarcastically

"Thanks" he sighed

"Your welcome Isaac" she smiled

"So what are we gunna do today Luna?" he asked her

"I don't know we could watch more movies" she suggested

"No I have had enough of movies for a while" he sighed

"Then what do you want to do other than that" she asked

"Uh......other than that can we do nothing but listen to crap music and dance around like idiots" he suggested more as a joke then a real suggestion

"why the hell not" Luna answered they both then went

inside Isaac put his normal style of two shirts on and they spend the whole day listening to music jumping around the room like six year olds loudly singing out of tune the songs it was quiet amusing to watch Luna at least knew the words and some sort of rhythm when she danced Isaac didn't he would just shout and scream words in the chorus he knew while jumping randomly trying to copy Luna failing abysmally this went on for quite a while till there was an extreamly liked song their favourite song came on to which they both stood jumping on the bed and singing the words loudly at each other only slightly moving on the bed they both knew every word that day really was just messing around after another few very loud very bad songs and jumping around there was a loud knock at the door they both looked at it a little confused there was no one around that would want to see them both, Jake was gone Andy was gone so was Mel even Julia had gone away for a few day's even though she would be back soon they were both very uneasy when the door knocked again Isaac jumped down from the bed and turned off the music "how's there" he said struggling to not panic there was no answer other then another loud knock at the door Isaac helped Luna get of the bed and they both walked very quietly towards the door as they got there Luna gave him a kiss then ran like normal when they didn't know who it was she ran into the bathroom and locked the door Isaac in hailed a deep breath before opening the door to see,

Chapter 21
his mother with Melissa and all four of his sisters they all basically pushed him out the way as they all walked into the room and stood around his bed all looking extreamly angry at him they all looked quite similar the only real difference between his sisters was the colour of their coat's each of them was skinny almost like they had anorexia and not really that tall he was taller than all of

them it was difficult by looking to see who was older the girls or him but if you had to guess you would probably think he was older then all his sisters but no he was the baby of the all he just watched them walk in before tapping on the bathroom door a certain knock they had agree to let Luna know it was safe as she came out and looked at the now large number of women in their room she then looked at Isaac he looked as white as a sheep again she took his hand and he grasped it really tightly

"W-w-w-what do you w-w-w-want now" he said

All his sisters laughed at him

"Look girls little issy's got his s-s-s-s-silly s-s-s-s-s-stutter s-s-s-s-s-still" one said mimicking Isaac's stutter as the rest laughed

"Oh but look he found some poor girl I bet she's only with him out of sympathy" another said getting an even bigger laugh

"oh but it's the big question we all want does issy's still have everything he left with" one asked

They all then looked at him curiously his mother looking as sour as ever

"Well issy still got everything you left home with" the same one said

"S-S-S-S-SHUT UP LILLY LEAVE ME ALONE" he shouted back at her

"Oh my god, issy found a back bone" another said

"Y-Y-Y-Y-YOU TO JASMINE" he said to her

"YOU WILL NOT TALK BACK TO YOUR SISTERS ISAAC" his mother said

"W-W-WHY NOT THERE NOT THE BOSS OF ME NOT JASMINE NOT LILLY NOT ROSE NOT DAISY NOT YOU NONE OF YOU ARE THE BOSS OF ME THE ONLY PEOPLE ON EARTH NOW WHO ARE THE BOSSES OF ME IS ME AND LUNA" he shouted back at them all Luna was almost shocked she had seen Isaac angry even if it was a rare occurrence but never this angry at anyone or anything "now what do you want" he added calming

down slightly Luna's hand now lengthened in his grip he
was to storm of she was gunna be going with him his
grip now ridiculously tight if he increased his grip any
more he was likely to brake her hand
"we came out here to take you home from this place to go
home and get a real job and have your life we planned"
his mother ordered sourly
"Did it ever occur to you I don't like the life you planned
for me" he told her
"it doesn't matter if you like it or not you are coming
home Isaac Richards" his mother replied
"Yeah issy" all his sisters said in sync
"im not going anywhere im staying here till my course is
finished and then god only knows where im off to im not
coming home to see the life you planed for me remove
what's last of my freedom" he explained
"You never had any Isaac, now pack your things before I
lose my temper with you" she ordered
"c-c-c-c-c-come on issy d-d-d-don't be a difficult
b-b-b-baby b-b-b-boy" lily said getting a laugh from all
the other sisters
"Yeah issy don't be d-d-d-d-d-difficult" rose said
"D-d-d-d-don't b-b-be a b-b-b-baby issy" jasmine added
"Hey shut up guy's I want to know what issy's lost since
he left" daisy said shutting everybody up it was obvious
that daisy was older than the others
"Yes I would like to know that to Isaac" his mother added
"Y-y-y-y-y-you really w-w-w-want to know?" he asked
"Yes" they all said the sisters sounding more mocking
where as his mother sounder very angry
"Fine I lost my glasses and my virginity okay" he
answered
"what" the sister's said before they all burst out laughing
his mother just glared at him Melissa still having not
said a word just looked at Luna like she was trying to kill
her using only her head
"Well it's for certain Isaac your tipple grounded now" his

mother said

"you think I care if im grounded mum im here and staying here, you are going home to wait and just see if I come back" Isaac said slightly increasing his grip on Luna's hand it was now causing Luna quiet a lot of pain but she didn't say anything then his mother stepped towards him and slapped him getting not much of a reaction out of him

"You stupid boy you are coming home even if I have to drag you there kicking and screaming young man" she said

"you are not dragging me anywhere for the last time im staying her with Luna till my course is finished then I will desired what I do so can you BACK OFF AND LET ME LIVE MY OWN LIFE" as he shouted he tightened his grip again making Luna almost screaming the pain she was in was unbelievable it was strange that Isaac had that much strength but Luna still didn't say anything all his sisters looked at him confused obviously in shock from his outburst Melissa still didn't remove her eye's from Luna but Luna didn't care she was busy looking at Isaac "now can you please just leave me alone" he said now almost crying

"I will not allow my only son to gallivant of on some stupid collage course with some cheap girl" his mother said

"She's not cheap she's better than any of them" he answered referring to his sisters and Melissa

His mother then slapped him again still not getting much of a response from him

"will you just go home" he said still increasing him grip of Luna's hand so much she had to shut her eye's to stop herself from calling out and with one more sharp look his mother left putting up hardly any fight his sisters each gave him a punch in the arm as they left Melissa just stood for a while before beginning to walk out she stopped for a second next to Isaac he didn't give her a glance but Luna basically started her down till she was out of view as soon as they were gone they both walked and locked the door and when and sat on the bed Isaac still hadn't let go of the extreamly tight grip till Luna spoke

"Uh Isaac I know you need something to get your anger out on but your kinda crushing my hand" she told him
he then realized and let go of Luna's hand
"Oh my god im so sorry Luna I didn't mean to crush your hand" he told her
"It's okay I know you didn't mean it, are you okay" she asked him
"Im fine" he said sounding very distracted
"Liar" she replied pulling him close
"I know im a liar I just hate them so much sometimes" he then began to cry
"it's okay I know" she said pulling him closer so that he was crying on her shoulder after a few seconds he stopped and she pulled him away just enough to see his face she put her hands on his face looking at where his mother had hit him "did she hurt you Isaac?" she asked
"No she didn't not this time, im sure she will be back though with more reinforcements" he sighed
"Well who else is there to get?" she asked
"The rest of the family" he sighed
"Joy that should be good, at least I'll meet your family" she joked
they then both laughed for a while then Luna got up and made some food it was like normal quiet quick they both wanted to go to sleep after that after they ate it they sat cuddled together on the bed "so what are we gunna do tomorrow" Isaac said
"I don't know, im sure we will find something else to do" she replied
"Well, any idea's" he said pulling her closer
"A few" she answered as she put her hands on his chest and he gave her nose a kiss

"Like" he said slyly
"Like going to sleep" she answered
"Ow" he complained
"Sorry Isaac not today" she told him
"Fine" he replied giving her another kiss
After a while of just lying in each other's arms till Luna
spoke again
"Hey Isaac?" she said
"Yes Luna" he answered
"What do you think would happen if you did go home?"
she asked
"I don't know and I don't care because im not going
home" he told her
"Okay fine, but what did you use to do before you ran off,
im just curious" she asked
"Well not a lot just doing whatever my mum told me to
do" he sighed
"What about you know, girls and stuff" she giggled
"well I had my sisters giving me orders all the time and
times my mum would tell me to go down the street and
see Melissa but it would just go around the corner for a
cig and that's about it oh and have all my bed times with
the bear" he explained
"Aww" she replied giving him a kiss" I bet your bear never
did that" she giggled
"You would be wrong my bear would often give me a kiss
goodnight because I would make him do it" he answered
"Aww that's so cute" she said giving him another kiss
this time lasting longer in response he pulled her closer
so there wasn't an inch between them then began kissing
her to it like normal got very hot very quickly till Luna
pulled away
"Did the bear ever do that" she asked
"Once" he replied but it did seem like a lie
"What about this" she said as she moved one of her
hands down from his chest to the top of his pants she
then moved her hand and kept moving her hand up the

inside leg of his pyjama pants

"No" he said rather quickly trying to keep eye contact though it was proving quiet difficult for him as he was laying

"I don't believe you" she said in reply

He then turned around and got the bear from under his bed and sat with it

"Don't believe me ask the bear" he told her Luna took it from his hands and pretended to whisper in its ear and she made the bear nod

"What did you ask?" he asked her

Luna ignored him still pretending to have a full conversation with the bear till she turned with the bear in her hands and she make it talk

"Hello Isaac I missed you why did you put me away" she said in a funny voice using the bear to mask her face

Isaac gave Luna and the bear a rather unamused look but continued to talk to the bear

"Because my lord I found a girl to do your job" he replied to the bear

"but I can do better than any girl come here and sleep with me Isaac" she said in a funny voice before making the bear kiss all over his face while she laughed at him till Isaac just snatched it out her hands "look im not down with that sort of thing any more I have Luna now okay, go find someone else to do that with" he said to it

"wait" Luna said getting up from the bed and stepping over to the other one she got her little turtle that use to sit on her bed till she moved into Isaac's she then got back into the bed and held the turtle Isaac laughed and turned the bear to look at the turtle

"And what's your name" he made the bear say

"peek-a-boo" Luna made it say

they both then made the toy's kiss before laughing like mad they then made the toy's cuddle and put them on top of the head board of the bed before cuddling together like the toy's themselves "we could learn a lot from them"

Isaac said

"You mean they could learn a lot from us" she replied

"Whatever so anything else we want to do tonight" he asked her walking his fingers up her back

"No just sleep" Luna said turning away from him to sleep

"Fine" he said wrapping his arms around her again giving her a kiss on the cheek

"Do I really do the bear's job?" she asked

"Well some of them" he answered

They then both laughed and fell asleep.

Chapter 22

first to wake up was Isaac he sat up to see the room like normal and Luna fast asleep beside him he got up and had his shower and got dressed before sitting on his desk chair slowly spinning on it looking at Luna sleep before getting up and walking out to go down stairs as he got to the ground floor he walked off to go and see Julia he needed to talk to her urgently he walked up to her door and knocked on it several times till she answered it she was like him awake and dressed already she let him she sat on her sofa as he stood for a second looking around before he spoke "I really need to ask you something" he said

"Oh why has Luna sent a message" she asked

"No she doesn't know I here look I know that's its probably privet information and stuff but what can you tell me about Luna's past" he asked her

Julia looked at him very carefully

"Why" she asked not in her normal tone

"Because im worried about her safety" he replied

"Well im sorry Mr Richards I can't give you that information" she said as she pushed him out the door he then ran off to the main part of campus where he knew no one was around and he got out his phone and called Jake

"Hey man" Jake said the sound of music and people

laughing just behind him

"Hey man I need to talk to you seriously for a bit" he said

"Sure give me a sec................okay go" during the pause the sounds stopped he obviously went inside

"look im terrified about Luna, I have even spoken to her aunt and she won't tell me anything about her past im just so sacred every time I fall asleep that she won't be there went I wake up" he explained

"hey,hey man slow down a bit you know Luna she loves you im sure the only reason she won't tell you is because it's not important look why not just calm down and go talk to her" Jake answered

"Your right Jake how's Harrison" he asked

"No, idea haven't seen him this morning" Jake replied

"okay have fun you guy's" he said before hanging up and walking back to the room when he got there Luna was still asleep in bed so rather than bother her he decided to make her breakfast it was mainly bacon the one soul thing he could actually cook without destroying it after a few minutes of cooking just before it was finished as the room began to smell of bacon he could see Luna waking up and slowly sitting up

"I smell bacon" she said

"Oh good morning to you two Luna, and yes I love you to" he joked

"Isaac shut up if you wake me by bacon you know you're coming second in line of importance" she said getting up and walking over to him

"Thanks" he replied sarcastically

"Morning Isaac, I love you" she said hugging him from behind

"That's better" he said smirking handing her a plate of bacon

She then went and sat on the table Isaac then joined her with his breakfast to by the time he sat down Luna was half finished they just sat in silence till they were finished

"Thank you for making food Isaac" she said
"Your welcome I was up first and bored so I made food"
he replied
Luna just laughed at him as she walked of for her shower
when she came back Isaac was just stood not really
doing anything he had obviously just been tidying up a
bit not making much of a difference to the room Luna
then sat on the bed and Isaac sat beside her
"So what we gunna do today" he said
"I don't know yet any idea's" she asked
"None what so ever" he told her
"Well I don't know we could watch some TV for a bit till
we get any better idea's" she suggested
they both then sat back against the head board of the
bed watching nothing of any real importance till Isaac
changed the channel and put the news on the screen
showed a headline about people gone missing from a
hotel in California they showed some pictures of some of
the missing people know one they knew till Mel appeared
on the screen in a swimming costume talking to the
reporter they just changed the channel they didn't want
to see Mel right now after a while they gave up trying to
find something on TV "this is madness over a million
channels and nothing on worth watching" he sighed
"I know but there's not much else to do" she sighed
After a while they just both sat on their laptops doing
nothing of any real importance till it was a few hours into
the afternoon when they both went out for a cig
they both stood watching the sun set sharing a cig just
talking about nothing really important till Luna
connected her hand with his holding it tightly she
seemed distracted for a while till the cig was done and
they both went back inside after they had dinner they
both just sat up looking at the celling for a while till Luna
turned so she was facing Isaac
"Isaac?" she said
"Yes Luna" he replied

"Nothing" she answered
"No tell me what it is Luna" he said wrapping his arms
around her
"I love you" she smiled
"I know I love you to" he answered
"I will always love you Isaac" she said
"I will always love you Luna" he replied
She then kissed him at it got extreamly hot turning into
much more then kissing till much latter they lay in each
other's arms both naked and tired.
Luna then turned to look straight at him pulling him
close to her making sure there was not a centimetre
between them
"I love you Isaac" she said
"I love you to Luna" he told her
They then both fell asleep.

Chapter 23
when Isaac woke up he walked of had his shower and got
dressed before walking back into the main part of the
room h as his eye's cleared from there morning haze he
looked around to see, Luna was gone the room was
empty other than him it had finally happened she had
ran off he almost fell onto the bed in tears looking at the
room she was gone without a trace he always knew she
was going but he didn't imagine it would be like this her
phone was gone so was her guitar and all her clothes
even her turtle was gone but she had left her movies and
her laptop behind after a while of looking at everything in
the room he noticed an envelope on her pillow he opened
it to see it was a letter that read:
Morning Isaac, I guess by the suspected look on your
face you know what's happened and yes I have run of
and this is a letter to tell you why. I needed to tell you
that no matter what you think I haven't run of because of
you this is not your fault and anything that happens to

me from now on is not your fault please don't think that. The longer I waited the harder it got so I decided yesterday morning to run off today and leave on a high note I guess I did that. I worked out it would only get harder to leave you the longer I waited harder on both of us. Now I know you're probably sat there crying your eye's out just remember im gunna be crying to for a long, long time. I told you once I had been running all my life and it's not quiet time to stop yet but trust me as soon as it does I will find you again. I mean after all this time all the changes I made to myself I was me when I was with you and all the plans I made when I first started running I never made a plan as to what to do when I fell in love, I guess I never imagined I would find you, but im so happy I did Isaac. No matter how bad you feel remember I am coming back for you and if I don't, then have the confidence to know my last though was you all the good and bad of you Isaac

also no matter what Isaac you are not to come after me please don't come after me you will only put yourself in more danger and if you did then I would never be able to live with myself if anything happened to you, for once in my life I have someone that matters to me and Isaac you matter to me more than anything.

Please don't forget me

Love Luna or by my new name Emily Jacobs

Goodbye Isaac

I love you.

and with that he began to cry like an idiot not sure what to do or how to go on without her till after around a few seconds he got up packed a bag of all his clothes and a few bits and pieces he didn't take his guitar or some if his bigger stuff he then left locking the door behind him he went to his bike stood in front of it wondering if what he was about to do was a good idea or not before getting on and driving away towards the city he and Luna visited once he thought if she was to pass though anywhere it would be there and like that he was gone from WestBrook without a trace to he was not listening to what Luna had said he didn't care about the danger he was going to find Luna and keep her safe till he wasn't able to do it and he drove off towards the city in a slim hope he would someday see Luna again....

20447898R00095

Printed in Great Britain
by Amazon